LOVE CONQUERS WAR

When the Earl had left Raina to take the Comtesse round the picture gallery, as he had promised, she went to the library.

But somehow the books did not attract her as they had done before and, instead of taking volumes from the shelves, she went to the window to gaze out at the garden.

She was still worried in case after all she had said to the Earl and all he had seen today, he would still insist on going away to some foreign country.

Then she would never see him again.

'How can he go? How can I let him go?' she now asked herself.

Then, almost like a dark cloud coming down from the sky, she thought that perhaps the Comtesse had told the truth – they were going to be married and then she would go with him.

It was then that she finally admitted to herself what she had actually known for quite some time – that she was in love.

She loved the Earl.

THE BARBARA CARTLAND
PINK COLLECTION

Titles in this series

LOVE CONQUERS WAR

BARBARA CARTLAND

Barbaracartland.com Ltd

ISBN 978-1-78213-158-8

THE BARBARA CARTLAND PINK COLLECTION

Dame Barbara Cartland is still regarded as the most prolific bestselling author in the history of the world.

In her lifetime she was frequently in the Guinness Book of Records for writing more books than any other living author.

Her most amazing literary feat was to double her output from 10 books a year to over 20 books a year when she was 77 to meet the huge demand.

She went on writing continuously at this rate for 20 years and wrote her very last book at the age of 97, thus completing an incredible 400 books between the ages of 77 and 97.

Her publishers finally could not keep up with this phenomenal output, so at her death in 2000 she left behind an amazing 160 unpublished manuscripts, something that no other author has ever achieved.

Barbara's son, Ian McCorquodale, together with his daughter Iona, felt that it was their sacred duty to publish all these titles for Barbara's millions of admirers all over the world who so love her wonderful romances.

So in 2004 they started publishing the 160 brand new Barbara Cartlands as *The Barbara Cartland Pink Collection*, as Barbara's favourite colour was always pink – and yet more pink!

The Barbara Cartland Pink Collection is published monthly exclusively by Barbaracartland.com and the books are numbered in sequence from 1 to 160.

Enjoy receiving a brand new Barbara Cartland book each month by taking out an annual subscription to the Pink Collection, or purchase the books individually.

The Pink Collection is available from the Barbara Cartland website www.barbaracartland.com via mail order and through all good bookshops.

In addition Ian and Iona are proud to announce that The Barbara Cartland Pink Collection is now available in ebook format as from Valentine's Day 2011.

For more information, please contact us at:

Barbaracartland.com Ltd.
Camfield Place
Hatfield
Hertfordshire AL9 6JE
United Kingdom

Telephone: +44 (0)1707 642629
Fax: +44 (0)1707 663041
Email: info@barbaracartland.com

THE LATE DAME BARBARA CARTLAND

Barbara Cartland who sadly died in May 2000 at the age of nearly 99 was the world's most famous romantic novelist who wrote 723 books in her lifetime with worldwide sales of over 1 billion copies and her books were translated into 36 different languages.

As well as romantic novels, she wrote historical biographies, 6 autobiographies, theatrical plays, books of advice on life, love, vitamins and cookery. She also found time to be a political speaker and television and radio personality.

She wrote her first book at the age of 21 and this was called *Jigsaw*. It became an immediate bestseller and sold 100,000 copies in hardback and was translated into 6 different languages. She wrote continuously throughout her life, writing bestsellers for an astonishing 76 years. Her books have always been immensely popular in the United States, where in 1976 her current books were at numbers 1 & 2 in the B. Dalton bestsellers list, a feat never achieved before or since by any author.

Barbara Cartland became a legend in her own lifetime and will be best remembered for her wonderful romantic novels, so loved by her millions of readers throughout the world.

Her books will always be treasured for their moral message, her pure and innocent heroines, her good looking and dashing heroes and above all her belief that the power of love is more important than anything else in everyone's life.

"War is horrible, cruel and devastates so many lives and particularly women's lives. I lost my father and both my brothers in two world wars and I know the feeling of despair and emptiness such loss can bring. Wars can only be stopped by love and only with love can women prevent more wars in the future. It is up to us."

Barbara Cartland

CHAPTER ONE
1818

Raina put her horse away in the stable, patting him because he had carried her so well.

Then she walked into the house.

It was a most attractive house with a profusion of flowers in the large garden that seemed almost blinding.

As Raina Locke neared the front door, she saw that a huge bowl of roses had been added to the table.

They were certainly beautiful and she smiled as she thought that Nanny, who still lived with her, enjoyed the flowers as much she did. She insisted on their being in every room in the house whether they were using it or not.

She walked to the door of the kitchen, opened it and called out,

"Emily, I am back!"

The cook, who had been with the Vicar for nearly thirty years, came out of the pantry.

"I'll 'ave your luncheon ready for you, Miss Raina, in two minutes," she began. "I be sure you'd be punctual and I've been wantin' to give you the news!"

"What news?" Raina asked.

She was wondering as she spoke whether it was a new baby who had been born in the village or else perhaps someone was near to death.

Her father, when he was alive, always insisted on being told the moment anything new happened locally and since he was no longer here, Raina had taken it on herself to visit the person afflicted.

"You'll never believe it," Emily continued, coming further out of the pantry, "but 'is Lordship's arrived at The Hall."

Raina stared at her.

"Are you saying that the Earl is back, Emily?"

"It's the truth. The postman told me that 'e called with a letter 'e had for Mr. Munn, the secretary, and when 'e delivered it, 'e tell 'im 'is Lordship arrived last night."

"I cannot believe it's true!" Raina exclaimed.

It was many years since the Earl of Monthurst had been in residence at The Hall and the whole village was, of course, part of his extensive estate.

He had been a soldier during the war.

When the Duke of Wellington had won the Battle of Waterloo, he had stayed on in France with the Army of Occupation.

Since that too had come to an end, they had been expecting he would return home, but not in such a sudden and unexpected manner.

"They must have been in a flutter up at The Hall," Raina remarked to Emily.

"That be true, miss, and the postman said they be practically standing on their 'eads rather than their 'eels, which be not surprisin' as' e's been away so long."

"He surely has and I look forward to seeing him."

"You won't be the only person a-doin' that," Emily smiled, as she went back to lift a saucepan off the stove.

2

Raina walked back into the hall and taking off the coat she had worn out riding, she walked into the dining room to wait for her luncheon.

It seemed incredible that after being away for five or six years the Earl should have come back apparently without notifying anyone of his intention – not until he was actually in his home.

They had been expecting him for so long that now he had appeared it seemed almost unbelievable and Raina wondered just how soon she would be able to get in touch with him.

Her father had died last year and there had been no other Vicar appointed to the village. They had a Service only every fortnight, when the Parson from a neighbouring village came to take Morning or Evening Prayer.

"You will have to wait," Raina was told when she had made enquiries, "until the Earl returns. The Church is on his estate and he pays the Vicar's stipend."

The same thing was said about everything else that was needed in the village and Raina knew that her father had a long list of projects that needed to be undertaken.

And he had hoped the Earl would consider them all favourably now the war was over and the Vicar had looked forward so much to the Earl's return.

Yet now her father was not here and Raina thought there was only her to inform the Earl of what was urgently required.

Everyone had suffered during the war and all the able-bodied men of the right age had been in the Army.

Although they had been pleased and excited to go, many of them had not returned and it had meant that there was a great shortage of hands to work on the estate.

The Vicar, who came from a large estate himself, had sighed as the crops were smaller and smaller each year and the weeds grew higher and higher.

The Very Reverend the Honourable Alfred Locke was the third son of a distinguished family who came from the North of England.

He had at first been granted a Living on his father's estate as was usual with several sons in the family.

But he had not got on well with his elder brothers and because he had known the present Earl's father when he was at Oxford, he had been delighted to accept a Living on his good friend's estate.

When the Earl had died a few years after the Vicar moved in, he had been very friendly with his heir.

But Clive had joined the Army as soon as he was old enough to do so and had distinguished himself in the Peninsula War and at the Battle of Waterloo.

Raina could not help thinking how disappointed her father would be not to be able to talk to the Earl about that battle and he had also been very interested in the Army of Occupation.

'Papa would have been so thrilled at the news', she thought as she toyed with her luncheon, 'but I am feeling rather apprehensive.'

The previous Earl had been very generous and kind to his people and he and the Vicar would never let anyone in the surrounding villages be in need or unhappy if they could help it.

Raina could not help wondering if the old Earl's son would be like him. She had seen very little of Clive even when he was a boy.

When he came home from his school, he inevitably brought a number of his friends with him and they rode his father's horses, taking part in steeplechases and Raina was far too young to ride out with them.

When she last saw Clive on what had been only a short visit before he went overseas, he had been nineteen.

Now he would be twenty-six and she was doubtful if he would even remember her.

When he was busy with his friends, they had no use for girls, especially for one like herself who was little more than a child.

She thought again about the long list of items that required attention on the estate and in the village as well as in the three other villages that were smaller, but they also belonged to the Earl.

If he refused to carry out the necessary repairs, the people would go on living in the discomfort and hardship they had had to suffer ever since the war started.

'I am sure that he will listen to me,' she reassured herself.

At the same time the reports from all over England were very bad and she felt it would be a miracle if they were any different here.

Raina had no idea whether the Earl could afford what was required of him and she could only pray that he would be able to help all those who were in desperate need.

When she had finished her luncheon, she went into her father's study.

She wished that he was sitting, as he always had done, at his writing desk. He took a great deal of trouble over his sermons and wrote them all out carefully before he delivered them.

He also kept a detailed account of everyone who lived in the village and recorded what had happened year by year in their lives.

Only this past year since he had died had Raina not kept up his record of local events.

She was wondering now whether the Earl would be interested in reading all that her father had written and she knew that, if he was interested, she had been rather remiss in not recording all the details as she should have done.

Then she told herself that it would be a mistake to worry him unduly the moment he returned.

The main problem where she herself was concerned was that, if she asked, as she had to, the Earl to appoint a new Vicar, she would then have to leave the house that had been her adored home ever since she had been born.

It had not been the Vicarage before her father had occupied it, as the previous Earl had not thought the old Vicarage large or comfortable enough for his friend. He had therefore divided into two cottages what had been the previous Vicarage.

These were then occupied by people in the village and he gave his friend this much larger and pretty house at the far end of the village.

The garden had been a delight to Raina's mother as it was very large and had already been well looked after by the previous occupants.

The house itself was very charming. It dated back to Elizabethan times, but had fortunately been modernised and now provided every possible comfort.

Raina had loved her home from the very moment she was born and the idea of leaving it not only frightened but depressed her.

There was that and so many other matters she had to discuss with the Earl and yet now that he was actually home, she was afraid of meeting him.

Supposing he would refuse to do anything that was needed in the village?

Suppose that he merely told her to find herself other accommodation as quickly as possible?

Suppose he would not listen to any of her pleas for those who were suffering?

Such thoughts passed swiftly through her mind and then she told herself that she was being absurd.

There was no reason to think the present Earl would be any different from his father, who had been a charming and generous man.

Yet there was another aspect that she had not really thought about.

It was that so many landowners simply could not, now that the war had ended, afford to do anything at all for their estates.

There was one particular estate not more than four miles distant, where the owner, when the war ended, had found himself practically bankrupt and he had in fact been obliged to sell his horses and his farms to whoever could afford to buy them. His house, in his own words, 'was falling to the ground'.

'Suppose that happens here,' Raina asked herself plaintively, 'what can I do?'

Her father, as the third son, had of course not been a rich man, but he had had a small income of his own and her mother also had a little money and Raina knew that she was better off than a great number of people, even though their dividends had dwindled during the war.

Her father's income had become much smaller than it had been previously and however she looked at it, unless the Earl was generous enough to give her a house, she most certainly could not afford to rent one.

Since her father had died, this had been worrying her and the subject was always at the back of her mind.

'Why,' she asked herself, 'has he been so secretive about it? Surely he should have informed in advance his secretary who has looked after his affairs while he has been away?'

But she had seen Mr. Munn only three days ago and she was certain, if he had known anything of his Master's movements, he would have told her.

'What shall I do? Shall I just sit here and wait or shall I go and call on him?'

She asked the question as if she was expecting her father to answer it for her and somehow in a way she could not explain to herself, she found the answer.

She should go at once.

She should definitely go and see the Earl before he learnt from others all that had happened, what was needed and what was expected from him.

Because she possessed a quick brain and was quick in everything she did, she ran upstairs and changed from her riding habit into one of her prettiest dresses.

Then, carrying a small hat in her hand rather than wearing it, she walked through the garden to where, at the far end it adjoined the Park.

She loved the Park which belonged to the big house almost as much as she loved her own garden and she had been fascinated when she was small by the herd of stags.

As soon as she was old enough, she rode with her father through all the old Earl's woods.

In fact she had often thought in the last year or two that she knew the estate far better than the new Earl did because he had been away for so long.

There were places in the woods that she found very precious, where she had ridden with her father, but now she had to ride alone.

There was a lake at the far end of the estate where there were excellent trout and there were trout also in the stream that ran through a number of the fields.

They were all part, Raina thought, of herself.

If she had to leave, it would break her heart because nowhere else could be quite the same. How could it be, when her father and mother were buried in the churchyard?

The memory of them lingered in every room in the house. In every twist and turn of the garden and, of course, amongst the flowers her mother had loved so much.

She had been feeling apprehensive before she left home and she was now much more so when she reached The Hall.

Built of red Elizabethan brick, it looked very lovely in the afternoon sunshine, at the same time very large and rather overpowering. It was a house that any man would be proud to own and to Raina it had always been a Fairy Palace which filled her dreams.

Now, as she walked under the oak trees towards it, she thought it looked even lovelier than it had when she first saw it.

Granted there were a number of urgent repairs that were waiting for his Lordship's return. Some windows at the top of the house were cracked and the bricks needed re-pointing in a number of places.

There were, she knew, ceilings that were stained by leaks or had split and fallen from lack of attention.

Equally The Hall was beautiful, it was historic and it was part of her dreams.

'I love you,' she thought as she walked towards it.

She crossed the ancient bridge over the small lake that was directly in front of the house and then she stepped into the courtyard in need of weeding and re-gravelling.

9

She raised the silver door-knocker and felt rather nervous at using it.

The door was opened after a short pause by the old butler, who had been there ever since she could remember.

"Oh, it be you, Miss Raina," he greeted her. "I haven't seen you for a long time."

"I have just heard, Barker," Raina replied, "that his Lordship has returned."

"He has indeed," Barker answered. "A real shock it was yesterday evening when I opens the door to him. For a moment I thinks he couldn't be real."

"Is he in?" she asked with some trepidation.

"Him be here and so I suppose you've come to see him."

"If he will see me, but he may be too busy."

"Him only has one guest with him," the old butler said, "and her be upstairs. So you will find his Lordship alone in the study."

"I thought that was where he would be."

She remembered the last Earl had always sat there and it was where her father had gone to talk to him about the village and the estate.

When she was older, he would come home and tell her all that they had discussed and how they had enjoyed having each other to talk to.

As she walked down the passage, she was thinking that, since he had been away at school or at the war, it was doubtful if the Earl would remember just how close their families had been.

Old Barker, as he had not forgotten the right thing to do, opened the door with a flourish.

"Miss Raina Locke, my Lord," he announced.

For a moment Raina felt as if everything swam in front of her eyes and she could not see clearly.

Then the Earl rose from the sofa where he had been sitting and she saw that he had a newspaper in his hand as she walked towards him.

He put it down and exclaimed,

"Are you really Raina? When I last saw you, you were very small and I thought rather obstreperous!"

Raina laughed.

"I have grown older and, I would hope, wiser. It's very exciting that you are back, my Lord, when you have been away for so long."

"I thought you had all forgotten me," the Earl said.

She mused that when she looked at him she would have found it hard to recognise the tall handsome man she was now confronting.

"I did wonder, when I returned, if your father was still at the Vicarage. If he was, I knew he would be able to tell me all that has happened whilst I have been away."

Raina was silent for a moment and then, as she sat down on the sofa, she said,

"I thought Mr. Munn would have told you that my father died a year ago."

"I am so sorry to hear that, Raina, but a lot of letters I should have received from England were lost in France. In fact, even after the war ended, everything remained in chaos, although it was not entirely anybody's fault."

"No, of course not, but, as I said, my father has now been dead for a year and the village, like everywhere else on the estate, has been waiting for your return to put things to rights, my Lord."

There was silence for a moment and then the Earl asked rather brusquely.

"What sort of things?"

Raina looked at him in surprise.

"You must have realised that just as France was so affected by the war, so were we. It has been very difficult for a number of people. The estate is *not* as you left it."

"I rather anticipated that," the Earl replied, "but I did not expect good friends like your father not to be here to help me."

"If it comes to that, I am afraid there is only me."

"What do you mean by that?" the Earl asked after a short silence.

"Many in this County have either left or become so impoverished that they have no money to spend on putting things to rights. Frankly, your estate is in a very bad way."

"How is it possible that good husbandry has not carried on normally in my absence?" the Earl asked.

Now there was an angry note in his voice and so quickly Raina replied,

"Everyone did what they could and I expect Mr. Munn did not want to worry you when you were at war. But now you have returned, I am sure that everything will be different, my Lord."

"I thought the house looked somewhat dilapidated when I arrived. But I have been too busy entertaining a friend who has come with me to look round properly as I suppose I should have done."

"It is not only the house. It is the farms, the estate itself and, of course, the villages."

"What is the matter with the villages?" the Earl asked almost aggressively.

"There have been no repairs carried out all through the war. The men who might have done them were away in the Army, many of whom have not returned,"

The Earl rose and walked across the room to stand at the window looking out and then he said without turning round,

"Are you expecting me to put everything to rights the moment I arrive?"

"No, of course not, my Lord, but I think when you look round and when you visit, as I am sure you will, the people in the villages, you will then understand what has happened while you have been away and do what you can to help them."

He did not speak and after a moment, she added,

"Papa did everything in his power. He also spent what money he had in keeping people from starving when they could not earn any money."

Again there was silence.

She wondered if she had said too much and painted too black a picture and so rapidly, in case he was feeling she was imposing on him, she went on,

"Everyone will be thrilled when they know you are back, my Lord, and I think you will find that just as they loved you when you were young they will love you now, especially if you help them."

"What you are saying is that I have to spend a lot of money."

Now there was a note in the Earl's voice that told her it was something he did not wish to do.

She could not think of anything to say and there was silence and then the Earl spoke,

"That is the truth, is it not? You want me back so that I will spend every penny I have on putting things to rights. You cannot blame me for wondering if I would find it more amusing to remain abroad rather than return to this country which, as far as I can see, has not enjoyed any benefit from our victories."

"That is not true," Raina protested. "We have been thrilled and delighted with the victories you have achieved over Napoleon and we are grateful to the men who have died saving us."

The Earl still did not turn and she continued,

"But, if you have suffered in the war, as, of course, you have, we in England have suffered as it has cost us not only our lives but possessions, homes and lack of food."

The Earl now turned round.

"I suppose because I was in France during the last three years I did not realise that. I thought, because we were not actively at war, that life would go on as it always has. And I would come back and find my home as it has always been – very beautiful and very comfortable."

"It is still very comfortable," Raina said quietly. "At the same time Barker and his wife have almost worn themselves out trying to save it from falling down, even though they have been short of food for much of the time."

"I cannot understand it. Munn had plenty of money to keep the estate going."

"I see that you have not yet talked to him. We have been heavily taxed in England. Even though we tried very hard to produce all the food that was required, which was impossible and also to repair all the buildings that were dilapidated, the Government took away what we possessed in taxes. That made everything we did far more expensive than it had been in the years earlier."

The Earl sat down again and sighed,

"You must forgive me. I really had no idea that things were so bad. Driving here from London I saw what the fields were like, also the cottages I passed. They were not on my estate and I hoped when I arrived here I would find that the situation was different."

"It might be even worse, but, as you can imagine, we have been longing and praying you would come home to resolve all our problems, my Lord."

Again there was silence and then the Earl said,

"Perhaps I should be frank with you and tell you that I have been thinking of leaving England and living elsewhere in the world, where for the moment at any rate, they have not even heard of war."

Raina stared at him.

"Leave us!" she exclaimed. "How could you? How could you possibly forget that your family has lived here for hundreds of years since the reign of Queen Elizabeth when they built this house."

She drew in her breath and went on aggressively,

"As yours is the biggest estate in the County, they have always looked to the Monthursts not only to lead them but also to love and protect them."

"I thought I had done my bit for England," the Earl countered. "I fought for six years and now deserve a rest."

"How could you rest if you knew you were now killing not enemies but your people's homes and the part of England they belong to?"

Raina tried to speak quietly, but, despite herself, her voice seemed to ring out.

Even as she spoke she had the feeling that the Earl was about to refuse her and she wondered frantically if he went away what she could say to all the people he had left behind, who were filled with hope and excitement because he was back.

Then, before she could speak, the door opened and Barker came in and walked unsteadily across the room.

She saw he was holding a silver salver in his hand on which there was a letter.

"This's just arrived, my Lord," he said to the Earl. "Although I tells the groom as brought it to wait in case there be a reply, he rode off."

The Earl took the letter from the salver and said politely to Raina,

"You must forgive me if I read this."

"Of course, my Lord. I would expect it is from one of your neighbours."

The Earl did not answer, but opened the envelope.

When he read the letter, he frowned.

"It is from the Lord Lieutenant," he said, "who I understand is now Lord Lewis. I think I remember him."

"Of course you do. He is a short, rather busy man, who your father thought did too much too quickly and did not attend enough to detail."

The Earl laughed as if he could not help it.

"That sounds very much like my father!"

He looked again at the letter.

"He welcomes me, having heard I am back home, although I cannot think who informed him. He says that as he is anxious to see me, he is coming to dinner tonight and bringing with him Lady Trowbridge, whom I saw in Paris two months ago."

From the way the Earl was speaking, Raina realised that he was not pleased at the visit and was wondering how he could put the Lord Lieutenant off.

"I am sure that Lord Lewis is only welcoming you because he is glad you are back," Raina suggested.

"It is not right for him to ask himself to dinner until I am ready to invite him," the Earl replied crossly.

"You could easily send a message to him to say it is inconvenient. At the same time you would find it difficult, as you have just arrived, not to be pleased by his attention."

"Well, I am not pleased and it has put me in an uncomfortable position."

He spoke angrily and Raina said,

"I am sorry he has upset you and can I do anything to help, my Lord?"

The Earl stared at her.

"Yes, I believe that you can. I suppose as we have known each other since we were children, I can tell you the truth without expecting it to be repeated to every Tom, Dick and Harry."

"Now you are insulting me," Raina retorted. "You must know that, as I am my father's daughter, if you ask me not to repeat anything, I will not do so."

"I am sorry, I take that back, Raina. Of course I can trust you, but I am in a fix and for the moment I am trying to think of a way out."

"Tell me what all this is about. I feel sure if Papa was here he would settle your difficulty very easily. Now I have had to do many things he would have done and I am sure I can do the same for you, my Lord."

The Earl smiled.

"That is exactly the sort of response I would have expected from a member of your family. I remember your father was very kind to me when I was a boy and your mother spoilt me with chocolates that always tasted better than any I had at home."

"That sounds so like my family. Now tell me what has gone wrong for you, my Lord."

She thought the Earl looked towards the door as if he was concerned that someone might be listening.

Then he sat down beside Raina on the sofa.

"To tell the truth," he murmured, "and now I am confiding in you, I came home hoping that no one would be aware of it. Or in fact be at all interested."

Raina thought he must be mad if he really thought that, but she did not say so.

He carried on,

"I have brought with me a lady whom I find very attractive and who is French. You will understand, as the French were so recently our enemy, I did not want anyone locally to be know who was with me."

Again it seemed to Raina it was extraordinary that he was not aware of his own significance. However, she prevented herself from saying so.

The Earl went on,

"When I was in Paris last month, I spent a lot of time with Lady Trowbridge. She is a great beauty and acclaimed not only in France, but, I believe, in London."

"Her name is always in the Court columns of the newspapers," Raina said, "and she is undoubtedly someone of great influence in London Society."

"I know that and so she will find it very strange and doubtless a good story to repeat that I am alone at home, except for my French visitor."

"How could you really think that no one would be interested in your return, my Lord?"

"I see now that I was a fool," the Earl replied, "but my friend very much wanted to come with me and, when I brought her over from France, it seemed safer to come here than to stay in London."

Raina thought he had been very stupid in imagining that people would not immediately contact him, but there was no point in saying so.

"What is worrying me more than anything," the Earl said, "is that when they come to dinner tonight, unless I can think of a way of stopping them, both his Lordship and Lady Trowbridge will realise that my French friend is staying here with me without a chaperone."

Raina nodded, but did not speak and he went on,

"You are well aware that they will not keep such a story to themselves. In fact it would then be discussed and laughed about in London by tomorrow evening."

He spoke bitterly and Raina thought that he must have suffered in that way before. Perhaps he had been talked about when he had what he hoped would be a secret *affaires-de-coeur*.

She could also see that it would be a mistake for him to be joked about in London before he took up his new position in the Social world as the Earl of Monthurst.

"What the hell am I to do?" the Earl asked almost violently.

"I think the only thing you can do," Raina said very slowly, because she was thinking it out, "is to have some other people to meet her and, if possible, someone who is staying in the house."

"You are right! Of course you are right! But where at short notice can I find these people?"

Even as the Earl said the words, he looked at her.

"Well, you for one will help me," he said. "And, of course, if you do move into the house, I suppose, although it would seem a bit strange, that you will be chaperoning my friend upstairs, who is, I should imagine, several years older than you!"

"That is not important, my Lord, but she must have a chaperone! If there are other people in the house, it will not feel as strange as it does to me at the moment."

The Earl looked at her.

"If I have shocked you, I am sorry. I realise I was a fool. I just thought I was coming home and that, as my parents are dead, there would be no one in the house. As the lady in question was very anxious to come with me, I thought that it would help me to find that matters were not quite as bad as they might be."

"But in fact they are much worse and now you are in a very difficult position, my Lord."

"I realise that," the Earl sighed, "but you have said you will help me. I am now waiting to hear how you can do so."

"I can stay here quite easily," Raina replied, "and Nanny can accompany me."

She gave a little cry.

"Of course Nanny can be the chaperone. She has been with us ever since I was a child. We often tease her and say because of the excellent way she talks she might easily be a Duchess!"

"I think I remember your Nanny. She bound up my knee once when I had fallen down and was bleeding. She gave me a chocolate she said would take away the pain."

"That sounds very much like Nanny, my Lord. She has always taken part in the Nativity play we have in the village at Christmas. I have told her she could easily go on the stage and be an actress."

"Well, what she has to do now is to act the part of an elderly lady who is chaperoning both you and my friend from Paris. We will have to get busy if the cook is to provide a meal for six people without any warning."

"Mrs. Barker is quite capable of doing so providing she has all the right materials, but you will have to send someone out immediately to buy the food she will want for dinner."

"Will you be kind enough," the Earl asked, "to go and talk to Mrs. Barker in the kitchen and see what she can manage to do? Then go home and fetch your own things – and Nanny."

He paused to draw in breath and then added,

"I suppose there is someone to make up the beds."

"If not, we will do it ourselves, my Lord. Don't worry about that, but go and find out if there is anything to drink in the cellar. They will expect to toast your health if nothing else."

"My health is now very much at stake, Raina, but if you will be as kind as you have been so far, then I feel that we will plough through the evening without my losing my reputation!"

"Which you will most surely do unless you are very clever," Raina pointed out. "I don't want to be critical, but it was rather silly at this very moment to bring a French lady back to England with you."

"As I told you, I thought I was being completely anonymous and no one would be interested in me in my own home."

"You must have forgotten, my Lord, how important your dear father was and your grandfather and your great-grandfather before him. You will find the whole family history in the library. I consulted it only a short while ago as I wanted to discover the names of your relations at the time the house was built."

"Why on earth should that interest you, Raina?"

There was silence and then he asked her,

"What is the secret?"

"You have your secrets and I too have mine," Raina said, "but actually I am writing a history of the County, and I would not want anyone to know about it until it is finished. If it is not good enough to publish, I would lose face."

"I am sure it will be a huge success and, of course, as you know, the library is entirely at your disposal."

"We have a good one of our own, although it is not as large as yours, but it is a little more up to date."

The Earl groaned.

"Now you are suggesting I not only improve the estate, the County and myself, but I also have to enlarge my library!"

"Well, I would hope you will bring it up to date just as you will bring the house up to date," Raina replied. "Now I will go to the kitchen."

She rose to her feet and the Earl also stood up.

"I am very grateful to you," he said. "I realise that, as you are almost one of the family, you are aware I have made a fool of myself, but it will not go any further."

"What we must do tonight, my Lord, is to prevent anyone thinking you are being foolish. You must instruct your friend upstairs to be very positive and say that she had run away from Paris because, during the war, she did not support Napoleon's endless wars and so was ostracised and abused by her French friends."

"Of course that is what she must say," he agreed. "You are very clever, Raina. I would never have thought of that myself."

"I am going to the kitchen," Raina said, "and please find someone to drive me home and wait while I pack my clothes and bring Nanny back with me."

"To hear is to obey," the Earl added mockingly.

Raina merely laughed, left the room and ran down the passage towards the kitchen.

CHAPTER TWO

Raina was driven home by a young groom she had known since he was born and he was very excited that the Earl had returned.

"Do you think, Miss Raina," he asked her, "'e'll be enlargin' the stables?"

"I would expect so, Ned. His Lordship is very keen on horses. But you know as well as I do that the stables need repairing and that will have to be done before they can accommodate any more occupants."

"If you asks me, there be a whole lot to be done everywhere," Ned replied. "Me mother's cottage be a real disgrace. The rain comes in and the windows be fallin' out from old age."

"I feel sure the Earl will see to everything, Ned."

At the same time Raina felt worried.

Suppose the Earl decided to go away immediately and then who would give orders for all that had to be done?

And pay for it?

Would he allow anyone to do so in his absence?

She had to think about the most pressing problems rather than those that lay ahead.

Having told Ned to go to the kitchen and ask Emily for a cup of tea, she ran up the stairs to Nanny's room.

At one time it had been the nursery, but now Nanny occupied it alone and had her few precious possessions arranged exactly as she wanted them to be.

She was sewing when Raina entered and looked up with a smile.

"Where have you been, dearie?" she asked.

Nanny had always called Raina 'dearie', as she had been such a beautiful baby.

"I have been to The Hall, Nanny," Raina answered. "His Lordship has returned and there is a terrible problem we have to solve for him."

Nanny put down her sewing.

"*We*?" she questioned.

"Yes, Nanny, you are vital to the solution of the problem and I know you will not fail him when he needs us very badly."

Nanny was listening to her intently.

Raina went on to tell her how the Earl had come back thinking he would be unnoticed and no one would be interested in him – and that he had brought with him a lady friend from France.

"Are you telling me she is *French*," Nanny asked.

"She is indeed, but she was in disgrace because she supported the English during the war and her relations are all very angry with her."

"That is as maybe, but I don't think we want the French here, not after so many of our men have been killed or wounded."

"I know, but equally, Nanny, we have to be kind to the Earl after he has been away for so long."

"Kind! In what way?" Nanny enquired.

"While I was there a letter arrived from the Lord Lieutenant, Lord Lewis, saying how he was delighted that the Earl had arrived home. He wishes to dine with him tonight and wants to bring Lady Trowbridge with him."

"I have never heard of her," Nanny said scathingly.

"Well, apparently she is very important in London, and, as her husband is a diplomat, she has recently been in France. And, from what I gather, she was rather infatuated with the Earl at one time and he has flirted with her."

"Who told you all this?" Nanny demanded.

"I guessed some of it," Raina admitted, "but you can quite see that the poor Earl, thinking he was coming home to be alone with his French friend, now finds himself confronted not only by the Lord Lieutenant, but also a lady who talks considerably and would certainly tell all London everything she finds at The Hall."

"If you ask me," Nanny said, "the Earl is heading for trouble. You know as well as I do, where a handsome man is concerned, no one keeps their mouth shut!"

"That is why we have to help him,"

Nanny looked at her.

"What do you suggest, dearie?"

"You and I are going to stay the night at The Hall. I am to be a distant relation of the Earl's and you a great friend of the family who is chaperoning me."

Nanny gave a sound of surprise, but Raina went on,

"That will stop Lady Trowbridge from suspecting there is anything unconventional about the party."

Nanny stared at her.

"I really don't understand, dearie – "

"Oh, yes you do, Nanny. You are a born actress, as you know yourself and you will have to be someone grand, so you have come with me to welcome the Earl home."

"You are suggesting that I am to act the part of the chaperone and be with you for meals and all that sort of thing?"

"That is exactly what the Earl wants and what you have to do to help him," Raina answered.

Quite unexpectedly Nanny laughed.

"I don't believe this. We have been sitting around here in misery all these years while his Lordship was away, wondering how we can keep the villagers from dying of starvation! Now he comes back and has a house party with doubtless champagne for dinner!"

"I would not be surprised, Nanny. It is what the Lord Lieutenant and Lady Trowbridge will expect."

"I think they should help him to get things straight before they start to celebrate."

"I agree with you, but we cannot let the Earl down and, if I stayed at The Hall without you, people would talk. It will be a great mistake for him to be branded a roué the moment he returns home."

"I think people would say a great deal more than that," Nanny murmured.

"Now listen, Nanny, you know that you can act the part if you want to. All you have to do now is to hurry and pack your clothes. You had better take some of Mama's because you will want to look really smart and you must wear that white wig you wore last year at the village fete."

"Are you really serious that I have to pretend to a lady of substance?"

"You have pretended to be all kinds of people at times – you are lucky I am not asking you to be a Chinese coolie or an Indian elephant!

"I am sure I could do those parts more easily!"

"Nonsense, Nanny. You know very well that you can play the Grand Dame better than anyone else. I recall you doing it in the funny little play we did two Christmases ago when you sang a song with the children."

"I remember it well and I had to look as if I was a grandmother."

"You need not look as old as that, but I thought the wig most becoming and if you take Mama's jewellery, or what is left of it, out of the safe, you will look very much the Grand Dame, which is what the Earl requires."

Raina jumped up and walked to the door.

"I am going to pack up my things now, Nanny, and please make yourself look smart and imperious. And you must think of a good name as both the ladies there tonight will have titles."

Raina thought for a moment and then added,

"Perhaps it would be better if you were just one of Papa's family. The Earl will not have heard of them. I just know that you will look like a lady!"

Nanny laughed.

"Your imagination is now running away with you, dearie, but I will do my best. However, if I am exposed, you will have to apologise for me."

"You know that no one can play a part better than you, Nanny," Raina smiled as she walked out, closing the door behind her.

She was aware that it would not be as difficult for Nanny as it would be for any ordinary nurse.

Her father had been a vet in at one of the villages nearby and had been very popular with the local farmers.

Being a good-looking man he had married above himself socially to a woman who loved cats and he was continually attending to them. She had been, Raina learnt, definitely a lady.

Although Nanny never talked about her childhood, she had been brought up to speak perfectly and without any trace of an accent. She had attended a school where she had met girls whose parents were wealthier than hers.

She had, however, when she was eighteen, lost her mother who had died during a very cold winter and so she had decided that, as she was bored with all the animals her father usually had in the house, she would seek a position looking after children.

She had tried one family where she was pursued by the Master of the house and, because she was frightened, she left in a hurry.

It was then that Mrs. Locke had heard of her and asked her to come to the Vicarage to look after the baby she was expecting.

The baby was Raina and unfortunately she was an only child and, because Nanny was young and devoted to her father and mother, she had stayed on.

Raina had grown up finding Nanny indispensable and when her father and mother died, she knew that she could not lose her.

"You mean everything to me," she said to Nanny only a week or so ago. "Whatever happens in the future, if we have to leave here and find somewhere else to live, I know I cannot do without you."

Nanny was very touched by the way she spoke.

"I was not thinking of leaving you, dearie" she had said. "We sink or swim together come what may, although I daresay that is not going to be easy."

"What you really mean is that we don't have any money," Raina added, "at least only a pittance and it will certainly not buy us a house as comfortable as this."

She had given a deep sigh as she looked out of the window at the garden and then declared,

"I love living here! I love all the flowers and I love walking in the Park and, of course, riding whenever I can in the woods."

"I know that, dearie," Nanny had responded, "but you have to be practical and I am quite certain that, when the Earl comes home, he will want to put a new Clergyman into the Vicarage and there is no house more comfortable and with all the amenities than this."

"I know that. Oh why, why did Papa have to die? We were so happy, even though I did miss Mama."

"Death comes to us all at some time," Nanny said comfortingly, "and I always think your father and mother, who loved each other very much, are together in Heaven."

"That is all very well for them," Raina remarked, "but if we are left in Hell, it's not so funny."

"Now you are exaggerating," Nanny had said. "I am quite certain, when the Earl comes home he will find us somewhere else, even if we have to go to another village."

"The people in this village would hate that," Raina said. "You know they look to us to advise them, to help them and to heal them! In fact there is nothing we don't do for them just as Mama and Papa did."

Nanny sighed.

"I know that, but, if the Earl does not want us, we will have to go elsewhere. As we have both got good and active brains, I am sure we will find somewhere without a great deal of difficulty."

Raina thought there might well be great difficulty about it, but she did not say so.

She had merely kissed Nanny and said,

"Well, as long as we are together, that is the only thing that really matters."

Nanny had smiled.

"I agree with you and we have to look on the future as an adventure. Actually it is about time you had one!"

Raina did not reply to Nanny as she had not been certain what Nanny meant.

But now she thought that if this was an adventure it was a very strange one and then it was not really hers or Nanny's, but the Earl's.

'How could he get himself into such a mess?' she asked herself. 'He must be stupid to have thought he could creep home and no one in the Social world would know about it.'

She was thinking while she was putting her night-clothes and an evening dress into a suitcase.

Fortunately she had a very pretty gown that she had bought only a year ago when she had been invited to the Hunt Ball. It was the first to take place after the war and everyone in the County was excited at the thought of it.

It was to be held in the Lord Lieutenant's house where there was a suitable ballroom, although Raina was well aware that quite a number of people had said it should really be held at The Hall.

That, of course, was impossible, not only because the house was more or less shut up, but because the Earl had not returned home. The Lord Lieutenant's house had been only just big enough, but everyone had enjoyed the occasion and so had Raina.

She had been introduced to a number of young men who were staying with friends in the vicinity and they all asked her when she was coming to London.

That was a question she could answer quite easily, but she merely responded,

"I am not sure – "

"Will you let me know if you do come?" more than two or three had asked and they had given her the address of their Club or their lodgings.

Raina had turned their cards out of her evening bag when she unpacked it at home and threw them away. She knew that there was no chance of her going to London and she was unlikely ever to see any of the young men again.

Now she wondered if perhaps she should have kept the addresses as, if she was turned out of the Vicarage, she might be glad of acquaintances somewhere in London, but she could hardly call them friends.

She finished packing her case and then she put it at the top of the stairs.

Next she went to Nanny's room to see if she was ready.

When she entered without knocking, she stood for a moment staring at Nanny, who had already put on her wig.

It was a very well made one that hid her fair hair and Nanny had put on one of the dresses that her mother had worn.

Combined with the white wig it made her look very distinguished and very much a lady.

"Oh, Nanny, you look marvellous!" she exclaimed, moving across the room towards her. "You must certainly be a Lady of Quality to impress the Earl's guests!"

"I think that's far too dangerous. They could easily look me up in one of your father's books and see that I did not exist or, if I took a real name, they would undoubtedly know the family and that would be a disaster."

Raina laughed.

"There's no reason at all why you should not be a member of our family and if you were perhaps an aunt you would be Lady someone or other and if they looked you up they would certainly find you really did exist."

Nanny thought for a moment.

"I met a number of your father's family," she said, "at one time or another. They are nearly all dead now and if they were alive they would be very old."

"I always forget Papa was the third son – as Mama once said, 'an afterthought'."

"I think that was true, dearie. It was because your family relations were all so old that your mother wanted someone young to look after you and, as your father was always so busy, to be a companion for her."

"Which you were, Nanny. Mama loved you and I love you too."

Nanny smiled.

"I was just thinking," she said, "as I dressed, that perhaps something will come of this. It is quite wrong for you, looking as you are, to spend your time talking only to villagers and having no real friends of your own age."

"I think we have said all this before," Raina sighed. "I have a feeling that you expect a Duke to drop down the chimney and ask me to marry him. And so then I will live happily ever after!"

"Well stranger things might happen and certainly his Lordship has dropped down the chimney when we had no idea he was returning, but it is a shame he has brought this French lady with him."

"You don't have to worry about her," Raina said. "What we have to think about is that the servants at The Hall must not recognise you, Nanny."

"There is no reason why they should. They are now too old to walk the mile down to the village and it must be nearly two years since I caught sight of them, let alone had a conversation."

Raina knew this to be true.

"That makes it easier, so now think, Nanny, what we are to call you. If you are to be a relation you had better be my cousin."

"That's a good idea, dearie. I am sure your father's family, the Lockes, can provide many cousins."

"Very well, Nanny, you be Lady Evelyn Locke and I will call you 'Cousin Evelyn'."

"That will do," Nanny agreed. "I hope no one will recognise your mother's dresses. I have taken out one of the best gowns for this evening and a different outfit for tomorrow, when I presume we are going home."

"Don't forget Mama's jewellery, you always said I was too young to wear it, but they will expect Lady Evelyn to be dressed up."

Nanny hesitated for a moment.

"You are quite certain you don't mind my wearing it?" she asked.

"Of course not, Nanny, you are as much one of the family as I am. If Mama is looking down from Heaven, she would be only too pleased for you to wear her pearls and, of course, the bracelet Papa gave her one Christmas, even though he could not really afford it."

Nanny smiled.

"He was always most extravagant when it came to anything for your mother. I must be very careful not to lose anything of hers, just in case you have to sell it later on."

Raina gave a little cry.

"Oh, we must not do that! I could not bear to part with Mama's jewellery. It is all I really have left."

"I know that, dearie, but we have to be practical. I have been wondering all night what we can do and where we might have to go."

"Oh, don't think about it now, Nanny. There are so many other things to worry about and we have to make the Earl realise how much there is for him to do now he has finally come home."

Raina paused for a moment before she went on,

"He seems to think he is very hard up."

"Nonsense, I am sure we would think that what he owns is a large fortune even though he believes it's a small one. But he surely has some money left and the sooner he accepts his responsibilities the better."

Raina thought Nanny was speaking as if the Earl was a child.

"Very well, teacher, you tell him what his duty is. I am feeling rather frightened he may be annoyed with us for interfering."

"Of course he may and he may ask us to move out at once," Nanny commented.

"Then what we have to do," Raina said, "is to make ourselves indispensable. I am sure if you play your part as the perfect chaperone, you will be asked again and again."

Nanny laughed.

"I think that's really unlikely, dearie, but we will do our best and no one could ask for more."

"I have packed my things. As you can see, I have changed into my best dress and, if it's not smart enough, I cannot do more."

"You look pretty and everything you wear always seems to be smart," Nanny told her, "even if you and I know it's threadbare!"

"Now come on, we have to hurry back. And before we step into the carriage, be quite certain that neither you nor I have forgotten your name."

"Lady Evelyn Locke," Nanny reiterated, "and it's certainly a step up for me in the Social world!"

"You look exactly as you ought to, Nanny. In fact, if you went to the village, no one would recognise you."

"I hope not and you must be very careful not to call me 'Nanny'. Even the servants at The Hall, although I have not seen them for a long time, might then suspect that I am not who I pretend to be."

"I will be very careful," Raina promised. "As there is no one about, we should carry our bags downstairs."

"Put them in the hall and tell the groom to fetch them from there. If I am who I am supposed to be, I would not soil my lily-white hands by carrying my own suitcase!"

Raina laughed and carried her own bag down the stairs and Nanny followed with hers.

They put them neatly in the hall and then Raina went to the kitchen to find Ned drinking tea with Emily.

"We are ready to leave," she said, "and our luggage is in the hall."

"I'll take it out to the carriage," Ned suggested.

Raina waited until he had disappeared and then she said to Emily,

"Nanny and I are going to spend the night at The Hall, as the Earl has some people coming for dinner."

"That'll be nice for you, miss."

"I am sure it has been a huge shock for him," Raina added, "to see what a bad condition everything is in. So when he asked us to stay the night rather than be alone, I thought it would be neighbourly to accept as he asked."

"Well, I thinks 'e'll have a real big shock when 'e sees what's been 'appenin' while 'e's been abroad," Emily answered. "Poor young man. It be a shame 'is 'ouse is fallin' down and from all that I 'ears everythin' inside be dusty and dirty."

"I expect Barker will have found people to wipe away the dust," Raina said. "But it will require a carpenter to mend everything that is broken."

"That's for sure and, if you're a-comin' back for luncheon tomorrow, you'd better let me know, as there's nothin' much 'ere in the 'ouse."

"I don't expect you'll be seeing us until the evening or even the next day, but I am sure, Emily, whenever it is, we will not go hungry."

"Not as long as I be 'ere, miss. I only 'opes that Mrs. Barker, who I've not seen for nigh on two or three years'll do 'er best for 'is Lordship."

"I am sure she will," Raina agreed confidently.

Emily gave a coarse laugh.

"I'll bet you, it be a real surprise when 'is Lordship walked in. I couldn't believe me ears when they tells me 'e'd come back. I thinks at least he'd give 'em a week or so to be prepared for 'im. Yet 'ere 'e be when we never thought it possible!"

Raina was sure that most of the village was saying the same thing.

Again she mused that the Earl had been extremely stupid. How could he think he could sneak back and no one would be interested?

Aloud she said,

"Well, I would expect by this evening, at any rate, everyone in the village will know his Lordship is back. I would not be surprised if they are on the doorstep in the morning with a list of grievances."

Emily laughed.

"I bet you are right, Miss Raina. We'll need an army of repairers to get the village lookin' as it did before 'is Lordship goes away to the war."

Raina knew there was no answer to this and so she just said,

"Goodbye, Emily, and look after everything until I get back. And especially please look after Dickie. I am afraid that the Earl might object if I bring him with me."

Dickie was her dog – a small spaniel who usually went everywhere with her.

Nanny waited until Raina was in the carriage before she joined her.

Raina knew that she was waiting just in case Emily came to the door and was astonished at her new look, but fortunately for both of them, Emily stayed in the kitchen.

The coachman was obviously somewhat awed by Nanny's appearance. He did not chatter away to Raina as he had when they came away from The Hall and Raina and Nanny were also silent.

*

As the drive had been so neglected, they bumped over several potholes before finally they reached the bridge and passed into the courtyard.

Because she was looking out for them, Raina was more aware of the dilapidations and the intrusive moss and weeds than she had been before.

But it was no use pointing them all out to Nanny. It was only time and money that could clear them away and make the house look as it should.

Barker greeted them in the hall and Raina said,

"Here I am back, Barker. This is my cousin, Lady Evelyn Locke, who has been staying with me."

"I am sure his Lordship'll be very glad to meet you, my Lady," Barker intoned in his most impressive manner.

"I am delighted to see this beautiful house, which I have heard so much about," Nanny replied.

She was saying, Raina thought, just what a grand Lady would have said.

As Ned brought in their cases, Barker suggested,

"This way, my Lady. His Lordship's in the study."

Raina let Nanny go first, thinking that she looked very distinguished.

They then followed Barker down the long corridor that led from the hall to the study.

Raina was glad that they were sitting there, as she knew that without flowers and badly in need of dusting, the bigger drawing room would have been rather depressing.

As she and Nanny entered the study, the sunshine was streaming in through the window and for a moment it was possible to forget the wear and tear that had left the room so sadly in need of attention.

The Earl was sitting by the side of the sofa and reclining on it was a very elegantly dressed woman.

She could not, Raina thought, be taken for anything but French.

"Your guests, my Lord," Barker announced.

"Oh, here you are!" the Earl exclaimed. "How kind of you to have come so quickly."

He was speaking to Raina and moving towards her, but at the same time his eyes were on Nanny.

"I don't think that you have met my cousin, Lady Evelyn Locke," Raina began.

"No, indeed," the Earl replied, "and it is very good of you to be my guest."

"I really think," Nanny said, "I should be thanking you, my Lord. I have been longing to see this beautiful house I have heard so much about, but I am not often able to come South."

"I am afraid that it is not looking its best at the moment," the Earl replied, "but, as you know, I have been away for nearly six years and a great deal has happened in that time."

"It has indeed, my Lord, and I think from what Raina has told me, you received a medal after the Battle of Waterloo. So I must congratulate you."

"I think everyone who fought that battle," the Earl said, "should have received not only a medal but a pension for life."

"I do agree with you, but that is the sort of idealistic action that unfortunately no government would agree to."

They had been talking a little way from the sofa and now the Earl turned,

"I must introduce you to my friend who is staying with me. She is the Comtesse de Morière."

The Comtesse held out her hand and both Nanny and Raina shook it.

She was, Raina thought, exceedingly attractive in a very French fashion and different in every way from the English.

Her hair was dark and her face was elegantly made up. She might have just stepped off the stage and she wore a great deal of somewhat flamboyant jewellery.

When she addressed the Earl, her voice was very different from when she spoke to his guests.

"You are very kind, *mon cher*," she said, "to invite these charming people to meet me. I was expecting when you brought me here to the country that everything would be very quiet with no festivities."

"It's just a small dinner party tonight," the Earl said. "I am quite certain, Lady Evelyn, that you will enjoy meeting our Lord Lieutenant if you have not met him already."

"As I have only just come down from the North," Nanny replied, "and we have been so quiet during the war, it will be a treat for me."

She spoke so naturally and looked so elegant that Raina wanted to clap.

She managed to say, as she thought it appropriate,

"My cousin was sad when she saw how much your drive had suffered from the war as well as The Hall itself."

"I well remember in the past hearing it described as exceptionally beautiful," Nanny came in, "but, as you have been away so long, my Lord, you can hardly be blamed for what has occurred in your absence."

"What has to be done not only to The Hall, but, I am told, to everything I possess is so frightening that I am thinking of running away immediately!"

Raina gave a little cry.

"You must not do that! Everyone is going to be so excited and thrilled you are back that it would be a blow they would never recover from if you deserted them now."

"What I am frightened of, Raina," the Earl said, "is people asking for too much too soon. In which case, as I have already told you, all I want to do is to run away and hide myself."

"You can hardly be a coward, having been so brave up to now!"

The Earl looked at Raina sharply.

"Is that what you think I would be?" he asked.

"Everyone might well think so, my Lord. Perhaps tomorrow or the next day you will allow me to take you round the village and show you the state it is now in?"

"I know only too well what I will see," the Earl said sharply. "I have no intention of raising people's hopes when they are bound to be disappointed."

"You cannot say that until you see exactly what has to be done," Raina persisted, "so please let me show you."

She thought the Earl was about to protest that that was the last thing he wanted.

Instead he suggested,

"I expect that there will be tea for us in the blue drawing room where I have asked Barker to lay it. Shall we move in there?"

The Comtesse sat up on the sofa and she put out her hand for the Earl to pull her to her feet.

"I find everything in your house so entrancing," she purred. "You are not to feel depressed, Clive."

She spoke in a strong French accent and her voice was very soft, low and caressing.

Then, as she slipped her arm into the Earl's, he led her from the room.

Raina realised that the Comtesse was making her aware that he belonged to her.

She thought that Nanny must be thinking the same, as they followed in a small procession down the corridor towards the blue drawing room.

It had once been one of the most attractive rooms in the whole house, but now it looked dingy. The glass of the cabinets that contained beautiful china was so smudged it was impossible to see through it.

Tea was arranged in front of the chintz sofa by the fireplace.

The Comtesse immediately took it upon herself to pour out the tea and Raina thought that it would have been more polite if she had asked the Earl who he would like to do it.

As Nanny was obviously a much older woman, it should have been her task.

However, the Comtesse was intent upon showing them that she was the one person of consequence present.

There were sandwiches to eat and also a rather dull-looking cake that Raina guessed had been bought hurriedly in the village. A few jam tarts on another plate did not look very appetising either.

The tea, however, was the best and Raina knew it was very different from the brand drunk in the kitchen.

The silver teapot, milk jug and the tray they stood on looked as if they had been cleaned in a hurry.

It was all very different from the shining silver that Raina was sure that the Earl was expecting.

She saw him glance at it once or twice and she was aware of what he was thinking.

'It serves him right,' she reflected. 'He should have let us know he was coming back. Then there would have been time for Barker to clean the silver and take on more servants. It's the Earl's own fault if he is ashamed of his home as it is at the moment.'

As she glanced at the Earl, he was looking at her and seemed to be conscious of what she was thinking.

Almost as if he was speaking aloud, he told her he had had no idea that he would have more guests than the one he had brought with him. And it was perhaps just lack of imagination that had let him do what would have been unthinkable for everyone else.

Raina did not know why she knew exactly what he was thinking – she only knew that she did.

As she was sorry for him, she said reassuringly,

"I am sure you have told Barker he can employ more staff immediately. Everyone in the village is longing to be here and ready to serve you as they used to do before the war."

"I am afraid those who were here in my father's and mother's time must be too old to work now," the Earl replied.

"Yes, most of them are," she agreed, "but you will find the younger members of their families will be eager to be up at The Hall."

"Then I must certainly see about it tomorrow, but I think Barker will have managed to find someone he knows who will assist him tonight."

"I hope Mrs. Barker has some help in the kitchen, my Lord. For two people just striving to keep themselves alive, it is rather different to instantly produce a delightful and delicious dinner for six people."

Despite herself, she could not help her voice rising a little as she spoke.

The Earl replied a little sharply,

"You have indeed made your views clear, Raina, and I will see that the servants' hall is opened up again."

Raina laughed.

She reckoned that he had scored a point, as it had not occurred to her that he would know that they had shut the servants' hall and locked it for the simple reason that Barker and his wife, with occasionally someone from the village, naturally ate in the kitchen.

She only hoped the Earl had been sensible enough to give Mrs. Barker enough money for the dinner.

It would break her heart if the dinner did not go well, yet it would be impossible for her to do everything without another person to assist her in the kitchen.

"After you left me," the Earl said, "I told Barker to send to the village both for food and helpful hands."

Raina smiled at him.

43

"That was what I was praying you would do, my Lord."

"Does it really matter to you one way or another?" he asked unexpectedly.

The Comtesse was now talking to Nanny and for a moment they were not taking any notice of the Earl and Raina.

"Of course it matters," Raina replied quietly. "For years everyone has been so looking forward to your return and hoping you would drop down from the sky like the Archangel Gabriel!"

She sighed and then continued,

"Then they thought everything would fall into place and be just like it was in the past."

"Did they really think that? I just had no idea that anyone cared one way or another whether I returned."

"You must be crazy, my Lord," Raina said almost rudely. "You are the most important person here. You are not only the owner of the estate, the farms and the villages, but also the Master of the people who live in them."

Her voice rose as she added,

"These people are your people and they look to you to save them from their misery."

"You mean because of the war?"

"Yes and because of your absence after it, when we were hoping and assuming you would come home."

The Earl did not speak and Raina went on,

"Of course your people who have always lived here are waiting now for miracles, which they are confident you will perform."

"Now you are really frightening me," the Earl said. "How can I put right the ruination of years?"

"I know the situation does seem overwhelming and perhaps frightening even to you, but for all the people who live here you are their only hope."

She drew in her breath.

"All through these years, they have been saying to their families that when the Earl returns everything will be different."

The Earl tightened his lips, but he did not reply.

Then the Comtesse intervened,

"*Mon cher*, you are neglecting me. I am sure you are talking about matters I don't understand, but I will try if you explain them to me."

As she spoke, she gave Raina a hard look that said better than words how much she resented the way she was monopolising their host.

Raina knew only too well that the French woman was feeling annoyed at their arrival and the fact that they were staying in the house.

"I wonder," she said quickly to the Earl, "if, now we have finished our tea, I could show Lady Evelyn the music room and in particular the picture gallery."

She smiled.

"We have talked for years about The Hall, but she has never seen it."

"Then I am delighted for her to see it now," the Earl replied. "I am sure, Raina, you will be an excellent guide, as you know far more about it than I do myself."

"That is something you must not say, my Lord, and the way to brush up on the knowledge you have forgotten is to walk round the house, remembering exactly what it looked like when you were a boy."

"I have already done so and it made me depressed."

"There is nothing wrong that cannot be put right," Raina asserted, "and you know that's true."

"Now you are bullying me once again, Raina," the Earl retorted, "and making me more determined than ever to travel to distant parts of the world I have not yet seen."

"If you run away," Raina said, "I will take that medal you won at Waterloo and throw it in the lake!"

For a moment she thought the Earl might be angry.

Then he laughed.

"You always have an answer, Raina, and I refuse to argue with you anymore. Go and show Lady Evelyn the house and remind her that it is not my doing that it looks as it does but Bonaparte's!"

He turned away as he spoke.

The Comtesse was holding out her hand for him.

"Come and talk to me, Clive" she cooed, "I have so much to tell you and you know how much I value your wonderful advice."

She was speaking in French and in the same soft seductive voice that made every word seem a caress.

As Raina and Nanny walked towards the door, the Earl's eyes were on the Comtesse.

He did not watch them go.

CHAPTER THREE

Nanny was entranced with the house as Raina knew she would be and she was thrilled with all the pictures, the furniture and the china.

They walked all over it, sighing when they saw the cracked ceilings and the faded curtains.

"I have never imagined in my wildest dreams such a wonderful collection," Nanny sighed. "In fact I did not believe such a place existed."

"I cannot understand why you did not ask Papa or Mama to show you The Hall," Raina asked her.

"It would have been a bit embarrassing when the old Earl was here. He did not like strangers at any time. Of course, once the new Earl had gone to war, we were far too busy for me to find the time to walk all the way to The Hall and all the way back."

Raina laughed.

"It's not as far as all that!"

"It is when you are tired from being on your feet all day as you know I have been!"

"That's perfectly true, Nanny," Raina agreed, "and you have been wonderful. Since Papa died, you have done the work of at least three people – and that includes me."

"You have been very good too, dearie. In fact you have been marvellous in all you have done in the village. They look on you as an angel come down from Heaven."

"I hope not, otherwise they will expect too much. I was never very good at performing miracles!"

"Well you will have to perform one now," Nanny said, "if you are to get this place made habitable so that the new Earl stays at home."

"I just cannot think why he is not as thrilled with all that he owns as we are," Raina commented. "But perhaps he will feel differently when he goes over the estate."

"If you take my advice, dearie, you will suggest or maybe surprise him by riding with him tomorrow morning. I am quite certain that French woman will not get up early. He is sure to want to try out his horses that I have always suspected have not had enough exercise since he has been away."

"You can hardly blame the grooms for that," Raina replied. "There were too few of them for too many horses. I have often thought that Mr. Munn should have hired more grooms whatever the Earl might say when he returned."

"If you ask me," Nanny remarked tartly, "that man should not have let the house get into the state it's in at the moment."

"I suppose the answer is rather easy. He did not dare spend the money."

"At least he could have informed the Earl when he was in France that more money was needed. It would have been far more sensible to keep half of the house in good order, rather than let the whole building deteriorate."

Raina did not answer.

She felt strongly that it was no use looking back and complaining about what had not been done in the past.

What they had to concentrate on was prodding the Earl to do things now, but she had the frightening feeling that he would not listen.

How could he think of going away when he was so desperately needed here?

So many people looked to him as a miracle-worker, who could wave a magic wand and then everything would be exactly as it was in his father's day.

'I will have to talk to him,' Raina reflected, but she knew it was impossible while the Comtesse was there.

Perhaps tomorrow morning he would want them to leave as soon as possible.

As they were talking, she and Nanny had now come down from the very top of the house and they were on the ground floor walking towards the Chapel, which was at the back of the house.

"I have not been here," Raina related, "since the old Earl died. He lay in State in the Chapel and all the people on the estate were told they could come and say a prayer for him before he was buried."

"I remember, but your mother was not well and I stayed with her. You went with your father."

"Yes I did and I was very impressed."

She opened the door of the Chapel as she spoke and then she stood horrified at the sight in front of her.

One of the windows had been broken and the rain had come in and soiled the cloth that lay over the altar.

It had also soaked the carpet, making an unpleasant mess and water was even dripping slowly down the steps of the Chancel.

There were weeds forcing their way up at the ends of the carved pews that had been in the Chapel for several hundred years.

"You would have thought," Nanny said, "someone would have seen that the windows were repaired."

"There certainly needs a very great deal doing to the whole Chapel now," Raina sighed.

She was staring at the altar where the gold cross had tarnished almost to black and the same had happened to the candlesticks.

She thought that someone with any sense, such as Mr. Munn, would have put the cross and the candlesticks away, but she supposed, as the Chapel was not being used, that no one had come anywhere near it.

It went through her mind that it might prove very unlucky that the sacred objects, which had all been blessed, should have been left in such a parlous state.

Perhaps God would punish the Earl for doing so and then she told herself that was the sort of thing she had thought when she was a child.

But what she had to do now was to make the Earl restore the Chapel to the way it had looked in the past and then at least those living in the house could use it.

She mused that, as the Comtesse was presumably a Catholic, she would not be interested in seeing the Chapel, but it was essential that no one else, and that included the people in the village, should see it as it was now.

As she looked round, she could see that everything was covered with endless dust and spiders webs and there were more weeds peeping through the bricks.

The other windows, apart from those behind the altar, were blocked with ivy growing outside.

Because Raina was really horrified at such sacrilege she wanted to go down on her knees.

She would pray that things would right themselves and that the Earl would not suffer, but she felt that Nanny might think it was strange.

She therefore prayed standing up.

'Please God help us, please,' she said in her heart.

Then, as Nanny moved away and walked down the aisle towards the door, she followed her.

"I think we should lock the door," Raina suggested, "and take away the key. Most people, especially those who live on the estate would be horrified if they saw that the Chapel has been so neglected."

She paused and then went on,

"They would undoubtedly blame the Earl for not giving instructions that it was to be kept in order."

"I am sure you are right," Nanny agreed. "It is a disgrace that any place of worship should be left in such a shocking state."

Raina did not say any more.

She merely locked the door and put the key in her pocket. At least no one coming from the village would be able to get inside.

She was determined to tell the Earl when she had the chance that, if nothing else was repaired, he must do something to the Chapel.

She could not, however, help feeling that he might laugh at her and would think that she was concerned only because her father had been a Clergyman.

'I must make him see that it is an important part of the history of his ancestral home,' Raina thought, but she did not speak her thoughts aloud.

"I think," Nanny said, as they now walked towards the front of the house, "that we should go upstairs and start changing for dinner. You will have to help me, dearie, as I have not worn an evening dress for years and I would not suppose that there will be anyone to help us."

"Not unless Barker has engaged housemaids. But I think he is more likely to have worried about someone to help him serve dinner than how we look."

"Whatever we do, we have to look our part," Nanny said. "It means you will have to inspect me very critically before I go downstairs and it would be a great mistake for anyone to suspect that this is a wig."

Raina nodded and Nanny went on,

"You realise I have to compete with the Comtesse, who is obviously very elegant and Lady Trowbridge, who I have read is an acknowledged beauty."

"What do you know about her?" Raina asked.

"Nothing but what I have read, but the newspaper described her as '*the beautiful and elegant Lady Lillian*', so I think we are in for a lot of competition!"

Raina laughed.

"It is quite obvious who is going to win, but we can be the 'also rans'."

"That is exactly what we will be, dearie."

They went into Nanny's room first, which was next to Raina's and on the same corridor as the State rooms.

It was obvious that when Barker or Mrs. Barker had time to attend to any part of the house, they had dusted and brushed only the important rooms.

As there were said to be over a hundred bedrooms in the house, no one could blame them.

Raina was only thankful that the room she was to use was very lovely, despite the fact that it badly needed a proper spring cleaning.

Nanny's room was exactly the same and they were named after distinguished guests who had stayed in them.

It was the Comtesse who, Raina discovered, had the best room of all. It was called after Queen Elizabeth, who was supposed to have stayed there twice during her reign.

Raina had not noticed, as Nanny had, that Queen Elizabeth's room was next to the Master bedroom where all the Earls slept with a communicating door between the two rooms.

She said nothing, but hurried Raina back into the room that had been allocated to her by Barker.

Her case had been carried up for her and Nanny's had been taken to the room she was occupying.

"Tell me when you want me to come and do up your dress," Raina suggested. "I am sure, Nanny, you will look magnificent in it."

"You now seem to have forgotten that my name is Cousin Evelyn. It would be terrible if someone overheard us and we were not aware of it."

"You are quite right, Nanny, it was stupid of me. As Cousin Evelyn, you now have to make the Earl realise tonight just how fortunate he is to have such a wonderful house. It would be committing an appalling crime if he went abroad and left it to fall into ruins."

"Is that what he is thinking of doing?"

"He told me that he wanted to explore parts of the world he had not yet seen."

Nanny was obviously shocked.

"You have to make him see that it's his duty to stay at home," she said, "and put this marvellous house back into the way it used to look."

"That is what I have tried to tell him, but I am quite certain he is not going to listen to me."

"You have to make him listen to you, dearie. Now that your father is no longer with us, there is no one else to speak up for the village."

She sighed and her voice deepened.

"I think that it would kill many of the people if they found they would have to carry on living as they do now, growing poorer and poorer every day."

"I know, Nanny, but how can I explain to the Earl how important he is – not because of his title, but because he is responsible for those who live on his land and who want to work for him if they have the chance."

As Nanny opened the door to go to her own room, she turned round and said in a low voice,

"If you cannot defeat that insincere, over-dressed French woman, then I am ashamed of you!"

Because it was such an unexpected remark, Raina giggled, but as she started to undress she felt that Nanny was right.

The Comtesse would obviously encourage the Earl to go abroad and then she would doubtless go with him.

Somehow, although Raina had no idea of how to do it, she had to make him understand that he belonged here.

'Surely his ancestors must realise more than anyone what he must do and they will have to help me persuade the Earl that he must stay,' she reflected.

She thought of the portraits of them on the walls in the picture gallery and wherever their spirits might be, they would somehow be able to communicate with the young man who had inherited all that had belonged to them.

'There must be some way they can reach his heart,' Raina said to herself.

She only wished that her father was still alive, as he could talk to him man to man and make him understand.

'You will have to help me now, Papa,' she prayed as she walked to the window. 'He has been away too long and has forgotten how much the English people look up to their elders and betters and, when they are as important as he is, rely on them."

She had often talked to her father at night when she went to bed and now she felt as if she could reach him, as she looked out of the window at the unkempt garden.

The grass on the lawns had grown high and all the flowers had been overgrown by weeds. Then, as the sun was sinking low in the sky, the shadows cast by the trees and the fountain, which was not playing, grew longer.

She felt as if her father was there and answering her prayers. He was guiding her, helping her and telling her as he would if he had been alive not to worry and that things would come right.

He had always felt optimistic and, however difficult things might seem, he had never allowed them to defeat him.

He had inspired all those who went to him for help with the same confidence and the same belief that God was there and they need not be afraid of being alone.

Then Raina turned away from the window.

She began to dress herself in the gown she had not worn for a long time and it was certainly very becoming.

Then she brushed her hair until it shone brightly and arranged it as her mother had always done – high on her head so that it revealed her long neck and white skin.

When Nanny came in, she was almost ready, except for having her dress fastened at the back.

Nanny certainly looked the part, Raina thought, as she crossed the room towards her, wearing her mother's necklace and earrings.

Her dress, which revealed the curves of her figure, might have seemed surprising on a woman with white hair.

"You look wonderful, Nanny!" Raina exclaimed. "I mean Cousin Evelyn."

"You look the same, dearie. In fact if we don't dazzle his Lordship's eyes, I shall be ashamed of us both!"

"You most certainly look the part you are playing, Nanny. In fact you look fantastic. I am sure no one who has seen you before would recognise you."

"I hope so. I am sure the Lord Lieutenant would be horrified at the mere idea of sitting down to a meal with a servant. There is nothing that Madame la Comtesse would enjoy more than seeing us kicked out of the back door!"

Raina laughed.

"I think she regards us as just tiresome intruders and is only interested in the Earl."

"That is obvious," Nanny agreed sarcastically. "If you ask me, the sooner she goes back to France the better."

"Well, that is something we really cannot suggest."

"Sit down, dearie, and then I'll do the back of your hair for you."

She arranged it differently, then stood back to look at Raina.

"If you don't win the jackpot, which is of course his Lordship," she said, "I will be exceedingly disappointed. You will have failed not only me but all those who are looking to you to make the Earl realise how vital he is here in his own house, if nowhere else."

"I will certainly do my best. But I have a feeling it's not going to be easy."

"You will win, dearie. Remember that everything depends on you."

"Now you are really frightening me, Nanny. Let's go down and I only hope the Lord Lieutenant does not say anything to upset the Earl."

"I am sure his Lordship thinks he has enough on his plate at the moment and it would be a mistake to give him any more."

Raina understood what she was saying.

As they walked downstairs, she said another little prayer that everything would turn out better than she feared it might.

The drawing room certainly looked more attractive with the chandelier lit and with candles on the mantelpiece and on the tables round the room.

The Earl was already there looking, Raina thought, extremely handsome and very smart in his evening dress.

When Raina and Nanny came in, he exclaimed,

"Now I really feel I am home. I remember this room packed with people when my mother was alive, all of them looking as smart and as beautiful as you and Lady Evelyn – "

"I am glad I am included," Nanny piped up, "and we do realise that this is a very special evening for you."

For a moment the Earl looked surprised and then he asked,

"You mean because I am home?"

"I think it means more than that," Nanny answered. "For the first time for years you will be sitting at the head of your own table, entertaining your own guests in your own home. I am quite certain that is better than anything the French can possibly offer you."

"When you put it like that, what can I do but agree with you?" the Earl remarked.

He glanced towards the door as he spoke and Raina thought he was worrying in case the Comtesse had heard what Nanny had just said and would be annoyed.

The door opened, but it was Barker announcing the guests.

"Lord Lewis, Lady Trowbridge and General Grant, my Lord."

As he finished speaking, the guests came into the drawing room.

Raina stared at the last man, knowing that they had not expected him.

He was a tall good-looking man of perhaps fifty and she vaguely recalled hearing his name during the war.

The Lord Lieutenant bustled forward.

"Welcome home, dear boy," he began in a hearty voice to the Earl. "It is delightful to see you and we have been wondering what has kept you from us for so long."

He shook the Earl by the hand and then added,

"Of course you know Lady Trowbridge and I must apologise for bringing someone you did not expect. But General Grant arrived unexpectedly today to stay with me and naturally I could not leave him behind."

"Of course not," the Earl managed to respond.

But Raina knew it was difficult for him to speak when he was being overwhelmed by Lady Trowbridge.

She was standing very close to him and one of her hands was on his arm.

"How could you, dearest Clive, have come back to England without telling me," she cooed.

She was speaking in a low voice and it was only because Raina was nearest to them that she could hear her.

The Earl did not answer, because he was shaking hands with the General.

"I did not expect to see you so soon, sir," he said.

"Lord Lewis told me that any time I happened to be in the County a bed would be waiting for me in his house. So I took him at his word when I had to be here today. I apologise profusely for breaking in on you without due notice."

"I can only say that I am delighted, sir. Allow me introduce you to Lady Evelyn Locke and, of course, you know Raina Locke, who is the daughter of Alfred."

The General shook hands with Raina and told her,

"Your dear father and I were at the same school together. Although he was older than me, he was very kind to me and we remained good friends all his life. I was very distressed when I heard of his death."

"He really died of overwork," Raina replied quite simply. "There was so much to do here during the war, and so few to do it, that Papa killed himself by always being on call. There was no one to help, so however much was demanded of him he never refused."

"He was always like that," the General reflected, "and I am sure they will miss him terribly in this part of the world."

"Of course they do, General, and so do I."

The General turned to Nanny and said,

"I have been acquainted with several members of the Locke family, but I don't think we have ever met."

"I have frequently heard about you," Nanny replied, "and how brilliant you were in the war."

"I want to forget that now. At least we have peace, but from what I can gather, peace in England is going to be just as difficult."

"You are quite right," Nanny responded, "and I feel that you, General, at any rate will know how to cope with it even if others fail."

Raina could see that he was delighted with Nanny's compliment.

She then looked to where the Earl was introducing Lady Trowbridge to the Comtesse.

It was obvious that the two women disliked each other immediately they came into contact, and there was a distinct sting in the way the French woman was speaking and Lady Trowbridge was being as unpleasant as she dared but in a polite manner.

"You must find it extremely strange after all that has happened these past years to find yourself in England," she was saying to the Comtesse rather provocatively.

"I very often came to England before the war," she replied, "and our dear host, Clive, was determined I should come back with him."

There was certainly no mistaking the anger in Lady Trowbridge's eyes as she countered,

"I think it is very brave of you. I only hope you are not insulted by the Englishmen who suffered so acutely at the hands of your countrymen."

"I may be French but, as I disliked Bonaparte, I was a supporter of the English," the Comtesse came back. "As a result I am ostracised by many of my French friends."

Lady Trowbridge, however, was not listening. She was speaking in an effusive manner to the Earl,

"It is so wonderful to have you back, dearest Clive, and you must be thrilled to be home again after being away for so long."

"We are delighted to see you," the Lord Lieutenant said in a jovial tone. "Lady Trowbridge was relating to me on our way over here that, when she visited the Army of Occupation, you were having a very good time in France."

The Earl frowned, but Lord Lewis went on,

"It was not a fortress as we in England thought it to be. In fact you had a good deal of fun in 'Gay Paree'."

His French accent was not very good, but the way he spoke and the manner in which he dug the Earl's ribs with his left arm expressed what he felt better than words.

"We also had a lot of work to do keeping our men from being bored," the Earl retorted. "Most of them were anxious to go home to what they imagined would be peace and plenty."

He spoke rather bitterly and Raina came in before anyone else could speak,

"There may be peace, my Lord, but there is also poverty and many people are hungry. That is what we are asking the heroes of the war to put right for us."

"Which is what we intend to do," the General said quietly. "But it is not going to be easy. We are depending on people like our host tonight to get matters back to what they were before the war."

"Quite right!" the Lord Lieutenant agreed. "In this part of the County we are depending on him to make sure that the men returning from the field of battle find a place in our fields."

The Earl did not reply – he was busy passing round glasses of champagne to his guests.

As there was silence, Nanny remarked,

"I am quite certain that if we can win in war we can win in peace. It might not be so exciting, but an enormous number of people do depend on what is done for them at home in England. It is a question, as it was on the fields of battle, of leadership."

"You are absolutely right, Lady Evelyn," the Lord Lieutenant said, and I am sure that the Earl will lead the way for us here."

There was still no answer from the Earl and Raina felt he gave a sigh of relief when Barker announced,

"Dinner is served, my Lord."

The Earl offered his arm to Lady Trowbridge to escort her into the dining room.

As she took it eagerly, Raina saw the expression on the Comtesse's face and realised that she was furious.

It was, however, the correct procedure.

Lady Trowbridge was the guest of honour, whilst the Comtesse was staying in the house and she accepted the arm of the Lord Lieutenant with somewhat bad grace.

Her eyes, Raina saw, were fixed on the Earl as he moved out of the door with Lady Trowbridge.

And this left the General, Nanny and herself.

"As I am the gate-crasher at the feast," the General pronounced, "you will have to forgive me by allowing me to escort both you ladies into the dining room!"

Nanny smiled at him.

"I think perhaps it is rather greedy of you, General, but I am delighted to accept."

"So am I," Raina said, taking his other arm. "I only wish Papa was here to welcome you."

"I wish so too, but I am quite certain you will take your father's place in showing our host where his duty lies in the future."

Raina looked at him in surprise as he continued,

"I had heard, when I was last visiting the Army of Occupation that he intended to explore the world rather than return, as everyone wanted him to do, to his home."

"So he has been talking about it for some time!" Raina exclaimed more to herself than to the General.

"I discussed it with him one evening after supper and he said that, after all that the young men had suffered in the war with Napoleon, he was certain that a number of them like himself would find it impossible to settle down in the quietness of the English countryside."

Raina wanted to cry out that if the Earl did not do so it would be disastrous to The Hall and the whole estate.

But it proved impossible to have a conversation as they had now reached the dining room.

She saw that Barker had laid an extra place at the table and, when they sat down, she found that the General had Nanny on one side of him.

She was on his other with the Lord Lieutenant on her left.

And this meant that Nanny had the Comtesse, who was sitting on the left of the Earl, on her other side.

Lady Trowbridge was, of course, on the Earl's right and the *placement* was how the Earl directed them to sit.

He had perhaps been a little confused by General Grants' last minute arrival and Raina now wondered if she should offer her seat next to the Lord Lieutenant to Nanny.

Then she realised that if she did so she would be sitting next the Comtesse and, seeing just how unpleasant she was, she shuddered at the idea.

It was obvious that the Comtesse was determined to monopolise the Earl, but Lady Trowbridge was equally intent on holding his attention.

They were both anxious to prevent him speaking to anyone else and it was made more difficult for the Earl as the Lord Lieutenant was clearly delighted to talk to Raina.

He had a great deal to say to her about the County and the conversation would have meant little or nothing to the other two female guests.

"I have been wanting to see you, my dear, for some time," Lord Lewis was saying. "But, as you can imagine, I have been extremely busy and I go to London frequently."

"It has been difficult for me too, since, as you well know, no one has been appointed in Papa's place. In the past, if anyone was ill or in trouble, they turned to him, but now they ask to see me."

"I can understand that. I am sure you do your best, but no one could be quite as marvellous as your father was to those in need."

Raina smiled at him.

"I am so glad you think that about Papa. So many people took him for granted."

"There has never been anyone like him," the Lord Lieutenant said. "I do so wish he was here today now that Monthurst has come home."

"I just hope that now he has returned, he will stay," Raina said. "Otherwise I cannot imagine what will happen to the estate and The Hall."

"I rather gather from what the General said to me that Clive was thinking of going on his travels and perhaps living abroad. Well, we have to put a stop to that idea and I am looking to you, Raina, as you will see him more than I do, to put the right ideas into his head."

"I will try, my Lord. Please do tell him how much he is wanted and I am sure he will listen to you."

"If I know anything about this family, they listen to no one except themselves. Your dear father was the same. He always did exactly as he thought right. And I must say now that, whenever we disagreed, I was wrong and he was invariably right. I don't mind admitting that at times he made me very irritated!"

Raina chuckled.

"When he made up his mind, it was no use arguing. Even as a child I knew that I had to do as he wanted and my opinion was of little significance."

"As I have said, your father was always right, so naturally you must be right too, especially where Clive is concerned."

He dropped his voice before he added,

"I was delighted to find that you were staying here and, of course, with one of your family."

His voice was just a whisper as he continued,

"I am sure a lot of people would be very shocked at his entertaining a French woman as soon as he came home. Lady Trowbridge has had a great deal to say about it."

"The Comtesse claims that she was on the side of the English all through the war and therefore we should welcome her now as a compatriot, not as an enemy."

She saw that the Lord Lieutenant thought that this was a lot of nonsense.

He said quietly so that no one else could hear,

"I take that with a large grain of salt!"

Raina smiled and soon their conversation became more general and it was impossible for the rest of the meal to talk of anything private.

Then Nanny, in what Raina thought was, as to the manner born, took the ladies away at the end of dinner.

There was no doubt that Lady Trowbridge and the Comtesse were speaking to each other with barbed words and they had quite openly declared hostilities.

"You must be very brave to come to England at this particular moment," Lady Trowbridge commented adroitly to the Comtesse, her voice proclaiming all too clearly that she thought it an impertinence.

The Comtesse smiled.

"I was fortunate enough to have our delightful and charming host to protect me. In fact it was my idea that I should come and see his home, while he was anxious that we should go on a trip to North Africa."

So Lady Trowbridge told her in no uncertain terms what she thought of that idea.

Listening Raina knew that war was now declared.

In fact the two women were so rude to each other in a polite way that both Nanny and Raina were unable to say a word.

Only when the Earl rejoined them were the smiles back on their faces.

Both of them were clearly determined to show how much more she meant to the Earl than the other did.

"You promised to show me your picture gallery," Lady Trowbridge purred, "and, dearest Clive, I could not think of leaving without seeing it."

"I am afraid that it's impossible at this hour of the night. As you can imagine, I have come back to find the house in darkness, because no one was living in it except for two elderly servants."

"No one else?" she exclaimed.

"I have already learnt from my butler," the Earl continued, "that every possible candle that is not needed in the bedrooms has been commandeered for this room and the dining room!"

"Then I will have to come and see it tomorrow," Lady Trowbridge said firmly. "I was hoping you would drive me back to London when I leave Lord Lewis. He has been kind enough to ask me to stay for as long as I wish. I really dread that lonely drive unless someone is with me."

There was, Raina thought, a distinct pause before the Earl found an answer.

Finally he replied,

"Of course, Lillian, I would be delighted to drive you back if I was going to London. But there is so much for me to see to here now that I have returned. Therefore I dare not make any new engagements until I know exactly where I am and what is expected of me."

Raina nearly applauded, thinking this was a very astute answer.

But the Comtesse spoilt it by putting out her hand and saying,

"You must not forget, *mon brave*, that I have come here especially to see your lovely house. And I have also promised that I will help you in the picture gallery, which I am told is in a bad state of repair and needs a very keen eye to save the precious pictures, which are so much a part of your history and heritage."

She spoke so pleadingly that again Raina thought that she ought to applaud.

"I have not forgotten that," the Earl answered. "Of course, after your kindness to me when I was in Paris, I can only invite you to stay as long as you can. I will certainly pick your brains on the restoration of the picture gallery."

The fury on Lady Trowbridge's face was, Raina felt, so expressive that she almost expected the Comtesse to fall dead.

Then, as if he knew that the knives were out and it was only a question of time before the two women were at each other's throats, the Earl suggested,

"I wonder if any of you would like to play bridge. I am sure my butler will find some cards for us."

There was silence for a moment and then the Lord Lieutenant came in,

"I think, Clive, as you have only just arrived home and after such a long journey from France, we must not overstay our welcome. I will call on you tomorrow and tell you about a number of issues I think you will find both interesting and depressing."

The General laughed at this.

"Do we ever have to do anything else?" he asked. "If you aim for the stars, you always find there is a trap waiting for you beneath them!"

He waited for the laughter and then he added,

"Lord Lewis is right. Lady Trowbridge and I will not presume on our host's hospitality, but hope he will ask us again on another occasion."

"Of course he will," Lady Trowbridge intervened. "He told me when we were in Paris, I would always be welcome, so I am sure, Clive, I can come and stay with you when I leave Lord Lewis."

"I will be delighted to welcome you," the Earl said.

There was nothing else he could say.

The Lord Lieutenant rose to his feet.

"I will ride over after breakfast and have a word with you," the General said. "I have to go back to London in the afternoon, but I must see you before I go."

"Of course. What time shall I expect you?"

"Oh, about ten or half-past," the General answered. "I will also insist then on seeing the picture gallery, which is apparently an El Dorado for everyone else here."

He glanced at the two ladies who were scowling at each other and there was a twinkle in his eyes as he turned towards Raina.

"You and I must meet again," he said. "I have a great deal to say to you about your father and I would also like to meet your charming cousin again, who I hear is staying with you."

"Yes, Cousin Evelyn will be with me for a little while longer."

"Then I look forward to my visit!"

As the Earl escorted Lady Trowbridge into the hall she and Nanny followed, leaving the Comtesse alone in the drawing room.

Only when the closed carriage that had brought the three guests to dinner drove off did Raina start to walk up the stairs and Nanny followed her.

The Earl closed the front door as there was no footman to attend to it and then he realised that they were retiring.

Raina lent over the banisters,

"It was a lovely party, my Lord," she enthused. "I think on the whole it went off well."

The Earl instinctively looked towards the drawing room before he replied,

"Thank you both very much, Raina. You were so helpful and it would have been very difficult without you."

"I only hope it is not so difficult now – "

Then, before the Earl could reply, she ran up the stairs and reached Nanny at the top.

"You were wonderful, Nanny," Raina whispered, as they went into her bedroom.

"It was fascinating, dearie. I liked the General very much. I am very sorry at the moment for the Earl. She is a horrible woman and it is not going to be easy for him."

CHAPTER FOUR

Rania woke early and remembered that she wanted to go riding.

She had put her riding habit ready last night and it did not take her long to slip into it.

Then she went downstairs realising that the curtains were not drawn. She was very certain that Barker and Mrs. Barker were sleeping late after the exhaustion of the dinner party last night.

She pulled back both the bolts of the front door, let herself out and hurried to the stables.

There was only one sleepy groom, rubbing his eyes when she appeared.

"Has his Lordship come out yet?" Raina asked him.

"Aye, 'e goes orf a few minutes ago," he replied.

Raina did not spend time talking, but hurried into one of the stalls.

She was glad to see a stallion she had ridden before when she had had the time. He was very fast and usually did not have enough exercise.

She started to saddle him herself. The groom came to help her, but she was really much more proficient than he was.

In fact it was less than five minutes later that she rode out of the yard, thinking that she knew which way the Earl would have gone.

She was not mistaken, as, after she had galloped to the end of what had once been the paddock, she could see him in the distance.

He was riding over heavy ground that had not been ploughed and she caught him up before he reached one of the woods. He looked round in surprise as Raina galloped up to him.

"You left earlier than I expected, my Lord."

"I thought you would be too tired to accompany me this morning, Raina."

"I am never too tired to ride. This is one of your stallions I have ridden before. He was very young when you went away so I don't suppose you had noticed him, but now I think he is the best of all the horses in your stable."

"If I had known that, then I would have ridden him myself!"

"You have plenty to choose from, my Lord, and the one you are riding is one of the last your father bought. Then he was only a few months old."

"I am delighted to find I have so many horses," the Earl remarked, "and I would like to have some more."

"Of course you should have *more*," Raina replied emphasising the last word.

He looked at her.

"I see that you are determined to handcuff me to the house and force me to do exactly what you want."

"You must correct those last words, my Lord. It should be what you want. It is *you* who will benefit from what is achieved here."

She looked round the field as she spoke and, before she could say another word, the Earl suggested,

"All right, go on, I know it'll please you to tell me."

"This field once produced a fine crop of wheat. I remember thinking how lovely it looked when it was ready to be cut."

The Earl did not reply and they rode on.

She knew that she had been right in thinking he was making for the lake. For him it had always been one of the more fascinating places when he came home from school and he and his friends would swim in it in the summer and skate on it in the winter.

They rode through the wood, which was so thick that they had to go in single file.

"You go first," the Earl said as the horses stepped onto the mossy path.

"On the contrary, you must show me the way to prove to me you have not forgotten how much you enjoyed coming here when you were young."

"I realise you are testing me, just as you are waiting to test me in the house. That is why I am avoiding being lectured by you when I get the name of an artist wrong or fail to recognise a fine piece of furniture."

"Now you are being unkind. You know I am trying to help you, my Lord."

"I hope you are speaking the truth," the Earl sighed and rode ahead into the wood.

Raina followed him, thinking how magnificent he looked on a horse. He rode better, she thought, than almost any man she had ever seen.

'Surely he will find this more enjoyable than riding some strange animal in an Eastern country,' she mused, 'or perhaps climbing a mountain with nothing to support him but his own feet.'

When they left the wood, the Earl thought that it had expanded considerably since he had been abroad, as now the trees almost reached the lake itself.

"The lake also seems bigger than it used to be," the Earl muttered, almost as if he was speaking to himself.

"Actually, it is," Raina told him. "That is why the wood is now at the very edge of it when it used to be some distance away."

"What has happened that it has grown bigger?"

"Papa thought that it was the flow of water coming down from the hills that has increased considerably. We had some very wet winters when all the rivers and streams filled up."

"I have always loved this lake," the Earl declared.

"I know you have, my Lord. The boat you used to row in with your friends is still in one of the sheds."

"I should hardly think it is safe now."

"Then you can buy another one," Raina replied.

His eyes twinkled as he chuckled,

"You never miss an opportunity, do you?"

"I hope not, for the simple reason I have to make you realise not only that it is your duty to stay here but also that you should enjoy it."

How can you be so certain of that?" the Earl asked. "If you think I would be happy living alone, you must be crazy."

"There is no reason for you to be alone."

She was thinking that any ordinary man of his age would want to be married and to have a large family who would enjoy everything he had enjoyed as a boy.

"I know exactly what you are thinking," the Earl crashed into her musing, "and the answer is *no*!"

Raina turned to look at him.

"To what?"

"I was reading your thoughts. You were thinking I should marry, settle down and have a large family. Well, it is something I do *not* intend to do and I will not."

Raina gave a little cry.

"Why not, why should you not want to behave like any man in your position?"

There was silence for a minute and then he replied,

"If you want the truth, I find women amusing for a short time. Then, when they believe they are in love with me, I find them, although I do suppose I should not say it, extremely boring."

Raina drew in her breath.

This was an obstacle she had not expected.

Every man who had returned from the war, whom she either knew or heard about, had been determined to marry the first pretty girl he met and those who had found employment of some sort were married almost within a week of starting their jobs.

As she was silent, the Earl looked at her cynically.

"It is unlike you, Raina, not to find a riposte!"

"There are lots of things I could say, but I feel you are not going to listen to them. The obvious answer is that, of course, you have not been in love, as we all hope we will be one day."

"I have often been infatuated, amused and at times delighted with some lovely creature, but I have known at the back of my mind quite positively that I had no wish to marry her."

"You have plenty of time to go on looking for the ideal woman, who I suppose is in every man's dreams and one day, when you least expect it, you will find her."

"I am prepared to bet I will not. My experience has shown me that what is called love is more often a short infatuation and, when one comes back to reality, it is wiser to move away as quickly as possible."

He was speaking sarcastically.

"We are not talking in the same language," Raina commented.

"I suppose, like all young girls," the Earl replied, "you think, as the Greeks did, that the other half of yourself is going to appear unexpectedly and you will live together in a Heaven of your own."

Raina knew he was referring to the Greeks' belief that, when God first made man, he was lonely, so he cut him in half. And then the soft, sweet spiritual half became the woman, while he was the fighter, the protector and, of course – the Master.

"Although you are being cynical," she said, "and sneering at the idea, I have actually known a number of instances where that has really happened."

"I don't believe you."

"I never tell a lie if I can help it. My father and mother were totally convinced that they had been together in many other lives and would continue to find each other when they died in this one."

She spoke quite simply.

Although the Earl wanted to laugh or at least argue with Raina, he found he could not do so.

Instead, after what seemed quite a long silence, he remarked sardonically,

"When I find the other half of myself, I will let you know and you must meet her, if I am not in Siam, North America or Timbuktu!"

"That is very generous of you, my Lord, and I hope you will pay my expenses in travelling to you, as I am quite certain I will not be able to afford it myself."

She was joking as the Earl had been.

Then, to her surprise, he asked quite seriously,

"Are you hard up, Raina?"

"That is something I want to talk to you about, my Lord, but there is no hurry and I suggest that our horses will be very bored if we don't let them show their paces on the other side of the lake."

"Very well. I will race you round it and, if I get there first, I will choose the topic of conversation and you will have to wait for your turn!"

Raina did not answer him.

She merely started off at a gallop.

They raced round the lake until on the other side the ground was too damp to race at such a pace and they drew in their horses.

Then the Earl declared a little breathlessly,

"I have to admit it was a dead heat!"

"That means our serious conversation will have to wait, my Lord. Instead I want to take you to another wood that is particularly attractive and is half a mile from here."

"Lead the way, Raina."

They set off again to another wood.

They must have been riding for two hours when Raina remembered that they had not had breakfast.

"I think we should go back," she suggested. "Mrs. Barker will be most annoyed if she has cooked you eggs and bacon and they are wasted because we are not there."

"As usual you are reminding me of my duty," the Earl replied, "when I was enjoying myself and forgetting for a while I should behave like the Master of the House."

"There is always – tomorrow," Raina added softly.

"You are right. I will look forward to meeting you and riding the stallion you are on today, now I know he is one of my best."

"That will be taking an unfair advantage, my Lord."

They were both laughing as they rode on.

She mused that when they returned to the house she had never enjoyed a ride more. It was so exciting to have the Earl as a companion and not to be alone.

That was something she inevitably had been when riding in the Park either on her own mount or on one of those in the Earl's stables.

She had often talked to an imaginary man who was riding with her, a man who, like her father, had found the woods, the lake and everything about the estate beautiful and enthralling.

But she had to admit to herself that she had enjoyed this morning's ride more than any other.

As they went into the breakfast room, Raina said to Barker,

"You must forgive us for coming back late, but his Lordship wanted to see the lake and the woods with the squirrels and the rabbits which were fascinating."

"I thinks that's where you'd be, Miss Raina. Lady Evelyn's had her breakfast and if you want her she be in the library."

"I thought that she would be there," Raina said as she sat down at the table.

"I just cannot believe that either you or your cousin have nothing better to do," the Earl smiled, "than to read some stuffy book that was written many years ago and has nothing to do with modern life."

Raina knew that he was deliberately teasing her, but she answered him seriously,

"If we cannot travel as we want to do with our bodies, then we have to travel with our minds."

"It is certainly a cheaper way of doing it," the Earl remarked, "but I think my way is the best."

"It all comes down to the same thing, which is if you can afford it!"

"Now we are talking about money again. I am sure it's a subject you are determined to discuss with me sooner or later."

Barker had left the room and they were alone.

"What I am really worried about is my home," she replied. "You know I live in the Vicarage and, although Papa is dead, no one else has been appointed as Vicar."

There was silence for a moment and then he said,

"What you are saying is that living rent-free in the Vicarage is for you the equivalent of an income which you do not possess."

Raina nodded.

"Because I have to think seriously what I can do in the future, I shall have to somehow find another roof over my head.

"I understand it's a problem for you, Raina."

Again there was silence before the Earl went on,

"If I go abroad, as I am intending to do, there is always room in this house for you."

Raina stared at him.

"Are you seriously suggesting that I should live at The Hall?" she asked.

"Why not. Certainly until it falls down over your ears. You are very pretty and I am sure that you will be married in the next two or three years, in which case your husband will doubtless have a house of his own."

For a moment she was too surprised to think and then she replied,

"Are you now telling me, my Lord, in a somewhat roundabout way that you are intending to leave England and live abroad?"

"I have not completely made up my mind what I will do, but I cannot for the moment see the necessity of taking on all the duties you have told me are mine, the most expensive and difficult of all being the restoration of the house and the estate. Not to mention giving your house to a Vicar whose sermons, thank goodness, I will not have to listen to!"

Raina stared at him.

"If you are not joking when you say that, then I can only say I think you are the most wicked and ungrateful man there has ever been."

"Why should you say that?" the Earl asked sharply.

"Because you were born into a family that has been admired and respected all through English history and you have inherited one of the greatest and finest houses in the country and yet just to amuse yourself you are throwing all that away."

She paused for breath before she continued,

"I suppose there is some obscure relation who will eventually inherit The Hall and who will know little about it and even less about the people who have lived here and respected your family and you ever since you were born. How could you be so – unkind?"

Her voice broke on the last word.

She jumped up from the table and, walking out of the dining room, slammed the door behind her.

She ran towards the library thinking she must find Nanny and tell her that the sooner they both went home the better.

She reached the library, but there was no one there, so she sat down on one of the window ledges and stared with unseeing eyes at the garden.

'How could he be so cruel,' she fumed, 'to all those lovely people who are so dependent on him and trust him? How could he throw away the house and the estate as if they were of no significance?'

Vaguely she remembered that there was a cousin to whom everything would belong if the Earl did not marry and have children.

The contents of the house were all entailed and so there was no question of their being sold, but, if they were neglected for very much longer, they would lose not only their beauty but their value as well and already some were past saving.

'How can he be so cruel?' she repeated angrily.

Then, as tears began to run down her cheeks, she searched in her pocket for a handkerchief.

It was, however, something she had forgotten and, as she tried to wipe the tears away with her fingers, a voice behind her said,

"I think this is what you want," and a handkerchief was pressed into her hand.

She had not heard the Earl approach.

She did not look round, but took the handkerchief from him and dabbed her eyes.

"Forgive me," he said. "I had no wish to make you unhappy. I thought that when we were riding together you looked more radiant than if I had given you a diamond brooch."

"I loved – our ride," Raina murmured.

"And I loved it too. So forgive me for upsetting you."

"Did you really mean what you said?" Raina asked.

There was silence and then the Earl replied,

"It was what I was thinking of doing before I came home and I was repeating more or less what I had decided was the only way forward for me."

He was silent for a second.

"Now you have made me doubtful, Raina. If I did go away, I would always be worrying that you might be unhappy and that the other people I have not thought about before were unhappy too."

Raina turned to look at him.

"Please come and meet the people in the village," she said. "Come and meet the people who think that you are wonderful and are going to save them. Then, if you do not understand what they and I are saying to you, you can go away perhaps with a clear conscience."

The Earl smiled.

"How could I refuse anything like that?" he asked. "Very well, shall I say, because I don't wish to upset you, I will not make any further decision until you have shown me what you want to show me and have told me what you want to tell me."

"You promise, my Lord?" Raina enquired quickly.

"I promise."

She smiled at him.

He thought that with the tears still in her eyes and on her cheeks she looked very lovely. Quite different from anyone else he had ever seen.

"What I will do," Raina said, standing up, "is go and change my clothes. While I do that, will you ask the groom to bring round the chaise? It is rather old and dilapidated, but it will carry us to the village. Then I will show you all I wish you to see."

"I will order the chaise, so please don't be too long titivating yourself."

Raina knew that he was teasing and without waiting for him to say any more, she ran down the passage from the library and up the stairs to her bedroom.

Nanny was there with a dress for her to change into.

She looked up when Raina appeared and asked,

"Did you have a nice ride?"

"It was superb. Please help me, Nanny, quickly!"

"What's happening, dearie?"

"The Earl has agreed to come down to the village with me. I must not keep him waiting in case he changes his mind."

Nanny saw the tears on Raina's cheeks and heard the fear in her voice.

She was, however, too wise to make any comment and she merely helped Raina take off her riding habit and put on a pretty dress.

Raina took a quick glance at herself in the mirror.

"Does my hair look all right?" she asked. "I have no time to fuss with it."

"You look very pretty, dearie."

Raina ran across the room and, leaving the door open, she hurried to the top of the stairs.

Nanny sighed and picked up her clothes and then she heard the door open a little further up the passage.

She was just about to shut her own door when the Comtesse, elegantly dressed and her face perfectly made up, stopped outside it.

"I understood," she asked, "*that* girl has been out riding and I thought I heard her come up here."

"Yes, she came up," Nanny replied, "but I think she has gone out again with his Lordship."

"The Comtesse stiffened.

"I wish him to take me into the garden," she said.

Nanny could hear faintly the sound of wheels in the distance.

"I am afraid you will be disappointed. I think my cousin has gone to the village."

"I understand," the Comtesse remarked, speaking in English, but with a decided accent, "she lives there. If she has gone to her home, I will miss the opportunity of saying goodbye to her."

"She has not gone home," Nanny replied. "In fact she is now driving with the Earl to show him how much our people have suffered while we were at war with your country."

"Not my country," the Comtesse snapped.

Now the tone of her voice was very different as she went on,

"Young girls barely out of the nursery should keep themselves to themselves and not intrude on gentlemen who have more pressing things to do."

"I think at present nothing in this country," Nanny said, speaking French for the first time, "is more important than helping all the people who have suffered in so many different ways from an enemy who, thank God, has been completely and absolutely defeated."

The Comtesse's eyes flashed.

"You are insulting me," she screamed, "and I will ask his Lordship, when he returns, to terminate your visit, which was, in my opinion, quite unnecessary."

She did not wait for Nanny's reply, but swept away to the top of the stairs.

Nanny, however, was smiling.

She thought the Comtesse was a most unpleasant woman. Not only because she was French but because she was trying to entwine herself round the Earl and she was clearly afraid that, if he had any other interest but her, she would lose him.

Nanny reckoned that she could be dangerous when aroused and there was something deeply unpleasant about her which she could not exactly put into words.

'I only hope,' she said to herself as she tidied away Raina's clothes, 'that the Earl finds out the truth about her before he becomes too involved.'

At the same time she knew that he was involved.

It was disastrous for a decent young man, who had been so brave as a soldier, to be caught by a woman who would inevitably do him no good.

*

As they drove to the village, Raina was telling the Earl, who was driving the two horses pulling the chaise, how brave the women had been during the war.

"Most of them were hungry," she related, "but they sacrificed everything to give their children enough food. Papa helped them whenever he could and there are at least a dozen children alive today, who would have died if he had not provided for them."

She gave a little sigh.

"We were all hungry at times and, as you can well imagine, we sold everything we could."

"It must have been infuriating for you," the Earl said, "to realise that The Hall was filled full of treasures of great value, but it was impossible to sell anything."

"I have often thought that and if you had been here you might have been clever enough to think of a way you

84

could sell a picture without the Trustees being aware of it or perhaps just one of the snuff-boxes."

"I wonder you did not try to do so."

"If we had done that, it would have been stealing," Raina said. "Papa would never have done anything like that. So we had no choice but to sell our own treasures."

She sighed before she added,

"We did not have many, but they went one by one. Papa spent any available money on the children because, like Mama, he could not bear to see them so white-faced and hungry."

As they drove into the village, there was no need for Raina to point out the dilapidation of the cottages.

And in those that were thatched, the occupants had covered the places where the thatch was missing with old and torn pieces of cloth or sacks and many windows had the glass missing in them.

Pretty gardens which the Earl remembered when he was a boy were filled not with flowers but with cabbages or potatoes, whilst some were nothing but dust and dirt.

There were endless broken gates and fences that had tumbled down.

Then, as they neared the one remaining shop, two women coming out of it recognised the Earl. They gave a scream of excitement.

Others in the road turned round and were running towards the chaise as the Earl brought it to a standstill.

"It be 'is Lordship! He be back!" one cried.

Then, as if by magic, people seemed to appear from every direction. Even those who were very old and had to be helped managed somehow to reach the chaise.

The Earl climbed out and started shaking hands as Raina explained who each person was.

"This is Mrs. Perkins," she said. "She has been so brave. Her eldest son was killed in the first month of the war and her second son at Waterloo. But she has managed to look after three other children who are orphans and they have all squeezed into her tiny cottage."

"It be terrible when it rains, my Lord," Mrs. Perkins said. "It comes straight in and, if we be sittin' in front of the fire, if we 'as one, we 'as to put an umbrella up. The place be often swamped with water."

There seemed to be a long silence before the Earl spoke and then he said,

"I will have it seen to as soon as it is possible."

"Oh, thank you, thank you," Mrs. Perkins shouted.

Then there were cries from everyone else and they did not wait for Raina to introduce them.

They told the Earl what was wrong with the pump in the garden, the floorboards, the roofs and, most of all, that there was no employment.

"My boy were killed in Spain," one woman said, "and we 'as 'is wife and two children to look after. But me 'usband be over seventy and can't do much as his legs be very bad. I does me best, but children want good food and we ain't got the money to afford it."

Everyone had the same kind of story.

When finally it seemed as though everyone present had told the Earl their troubles, Raina suggested,

"I think you should all be quiet for a moment while his Lordship tells you his plans for the future."

She spoke almost defiantly, but her voice was soft.

As she looked at the Earl, he understood it was a challenge and that he had to commit himself one way or another.

For a moment they just looked at each other and then the Earl began,

"Miss Raina has already told me how you have all suffered. But I can promise you that I will do what I can to help you in the future. Sadly I cannot bring back your men who died for their King and country and who had made it possible for us to remain free and not be slaves of France or any other country in Europe."

He paused and looked round before he added,

"But I promise you that you and your children will be looked after and will not go on suffering as you are at present."

When he had finished speaking, they cheered and a number of them rushed forward to shake him by the hand.

"Thank you, your Lordship, thank you," they said.

"We knew you wouldn't fail us," one man cried, "and we be proud to belong to you."

As they drove back to The Hall, Raina remarked,

"I just knew when you saw them that you would understand."

"I not only understand, Raina, but I am now rather ashamed of myself for wanting to run away. I suppose that was really why I thought of living abroad rather than here."

"Now you will stay, my Lord?"

"For the moment at any rate," he replied.

It was quite obvious that he did not wish to say any more and Raina deliberately did not press him.

She just wondered if he meant to restore the village to some form of prosperity and then slip off.

At least that would give her some time to make him understand that it was his home and surely he would be happier here than in any other part of the world.

It seemed obvious, but she knew he had not finally decided what he should do.

As they reached the gates, she suggested,

"Drive on to the other end of the village. I want you to see where I live and where I have been so very happy with my father and mother."

The Earl did not argue – he merely drove on.

Then, when he saw the pretty house with its pink bricks, the very same colour as The Hall, he knew without asking that it was where Raina lived.

The drive was a short one and the garden was filled with flowers that were lovelier than anything to be seen at The Hall.

As the Earl brought the horses to a standstill, Raina proposed,

"I would like you to come in, but, if you are in a hurry, you can just see how beautiful my Mama made the garden and why this means so much to me."

"The flowers are fantastic," the Earl said. "I cannot see why my garden is filled with nothing but weeds."

"You know the answer without my saying it, my Lord. Your grandfather employed eight gardeners and at the moment you have just one, who can do little more than provide enough vegetables to keep Mrs. Barker supplied."

She saw that the Earl was listening and went on,

"They too have often been hungry for lack of other food. It is not always easy to trap rabbits in the winter or to catch fish in the streams."

The Earl drew in his breath.

"I cannot understand," he sighed, "why I did not realise all this when I was in France."

"I expect that the French suffered too, but from all I hear, the Army of Occupation was well supplied and the soldiers had their regular wages to spend."

"I did not appreciate that things were as bad as this. You have to believe me, Raina, when I tell you I had no idea that people were really hungry."

"I think, although it might upset you, my Lord, you should see the notes that Papa kept of all that happened in the village during the war. He made a list of the people who died and those who were desperately ill but had no attention. It was very hard to get a doctor to see anyone."

Raina's voice deepened as she continued,

"Although Mama did her best, she could not cure everyone and what they really needed was simply food."

The Earl said nothing and then he turned the horses round and drove back the way they had come.

He went up the drive very quickly and stopped at the front door, where, as Raina expected, one of the new grooms who had just been engaged was waiting to take the horses.

Raina got out on her side of the chaise and the Earl on his.

Then, to her surprise, he walked ahead of her into the house without waiting for her or saying anything.

She had the feeling that he was angry.

As she reached the hall, she realised he had gone to the secretary's room where Mr. Munn was working.

She had always thought that Mr. Munn was a rather stupid man, who was afraid of losing his position and he had therefore, she was quite certain, not told the Earl how bad things were.

Yet undoubtedly, after his father's death, the Earl had not provided the money which he should have done and that was why the people had suffered so much as the war dragged on and on.

As the situation grew worse, there had been no one to turn to, no one except her father to help them.

She thought this was not the moment, but definitely sooner or later she would tell the Earl how much of his own money her father had spent.

But even he had not, as he might well have done, ensured that the Earl provided more money than had been arranged before he left for Spain.

'It's no use living in the past,' Raina said to herself as she walked into The Hall. 'But at last something will be done for the future.'

Then she went into the study, thinking that perhaps Nanny would be there.

To her surprise she found that she was and with her was the General.

He smiled at Raina.

"I hear that you have been taking the Earl round the village. Lord Lewis was telling me only last night how much the people in this area have suffered. I am afraid it is much the same all over the country."

"I thought perhaps we were worse than anywhere else," Raina said.

"War is war," the General replied, "and I would like to say that no one has ever benefitted by war at any time."

"I am sure that's true," Nanny came in. "Even the victors have lost a lot of men."

"You are quite right. I have always hated war and have even felt sorry for the enemy. But I suppose there are always people who will want what someone else owns."

"That is correct," Nanny murmured.

"I want to forget it all now and I am retiring from the Army."

"Surely you are not doing that!" Nanny exclaimed, "not when they need you to build up the peace."

"I think that I could do it better in Whitehall than anywhere else," the General replied. "At the same time I want a little peace and quiet. So I am thinking, although I have been offered a place in the War Office, of retiring altogether and settling down in my home in Dorset."

"That sounds very nice," Nanny said. "And, as a General, you have certainly played your part gallantly and they should ask no more of you."

"That's just what I think," the General exclaimed. "Perhaps you can help me, Lady Evelyn, to make the right decision."

"I think only you can do that," Nanny replied.

"I would be most interested in your opinion."

It was very obvious from the way he was looking at Nanny that the General was admiring her and enjoying their conversation.

Raina felt she was somehow superfluous and so she left the room, saying that she was looking for the Earl.

She walked back towards the hall and, seeing only Barker there, she went into the drawing room.

Seated in one of the comfortable chairs and looking extremely elegant and, Raina had to admit, beautiful, was the Comtesse.

Raina wished she had stayed with Nanny, but she thought it would be too obvious if she now withdrew.

She therefore walked on.

"Good morning," Raina began. "I hope you have found everything you wanted."

The Comtesse did not reply and she went on,

"I had to take the Earl to see the village. But he is back now."

"I rather gather that you were monopolising him," the Comtesse said in French. "And I want to make it quite clear, Miss Locke, that the Earl belongs to me and very shortly, although it is a secret at the moment, we intend to be married."

Raina stared at her, but could not think of anything to say.

"It's a secret," the Comtesse went on, "for reasons of our own. But, as I have told you, leave him alone and do *not* interfere. He is mine and I find the way you are running after him extremely unpleasant!"

She rose as she spoke and walked towards the door.

She had been speaking in French and the words had seemed to have a snarl about them that made Raina aware of how angry she was.

As the Comtesse sailed out through the drawing room door, Raina could only draw in her breath.

So that was obviously the reason why the Earl did not want to settle down and why he wished to live abroad.

When he said that he had no intention of marrying, he had been lying.

'How can he be so foolish,' Raina asked herself, 'as to marry a Frenchwoman? And one who will try to make him forget England altogether.'

CHAPTER FIVE

The Comtesse found the Earl and they disappeared until luncheon time.

Knowing that she was not wanted, Raina went into the library and looked through the books she had not yet read about the history of The Hall.

There were several of them, some very old, and she was fascinated by the number of distinguished people who had been entertained at one time or another in the house.

Queens, Presidents, Rulers from abroad and what seemed to her to be half the aristocracy of England. There had been balls, shoots, steeplechases and garden parties.

In fact everything she had never known because she had grown up during the war.

'It must have been so lovely,' she fantasised. 'And if only the Earl could make it as it was in those days, how happy everyone would be!'

When she thought about him, she remembered only too vividly what the Comtesse had said to her and she was suddenly afraid for him as well as for the people who relied on him.

'The Comtesse is a bad woman, but how can I tell him so?' she asked herself. 'He would only be angry with me for interfering.'

Once again she found herself praying to her father and mother. They would understand that something must be done about the Earl.

'Please help me, Papa,' she prayed. 'You know so well how much it means to all the people you cared for."

She must have prayed for a long time.

When she opened her eyes, she saw by the clock on the mantelpiece that it was almost time for luncheon and she then carefully put back all the books she had taken out of the shelves.

Everything was dusty and she knew that she would have to wash her hands before luncheon.

There was a cloakroom down the passage and she slipped in there. She was relieved to find that Barker had put out clean towels for anyone who wanted to use it.

Then, as she came out, she saw the Earl coming from his study. He was alone and she smiled at him and asked,

"Have you been busy, my Lord?"

She felt as she spoke that it was a rather tactless question, since obviously the Comtesse had now attached herself to him.

"I have been talking to Munn," he confided, "and finding out why it was impossible for him to do anything about the estate while I was away."

"Did he tell you there was no money?"

"He told me that and a number of other things and, of course, how marvellous your father was."

"Papa gave the people everything he could," Raina sighed, "but unfortunately it was not enough."

The Earl did not answer and by this time they had reached the drawing room where Raina suspected that the Comtesse would be lurking.

And it would doubtless be a most uncomfortable meal if she had anything to do with it.

When they entered the drawing room, she found to her relief that Nanny was there and so was the General.

"Good morning," the Earl greeted him. "I had no idea, General, that you were here."

"I said last night that I intended to come back this morning and here I am, although a little late. I am hoping that you will ask me to have luncheon with you."

The Earl laughed.

"Of course I am, General. I only hope there will be enough for us all."

"You need not worry," Nanny said. "Barker heard the conversation last night and had already suspected that the General would come for luncheon."

The Earl laughed again.

"I just cannot think how we would manage without Barker and I am very pleased to see you, General."

"I am delighted to be here," the General replied. "Lady Evelyn has taken me round the picture gallery which is even more splendid that I expected it to be."

"I am afraid there is a great deal to be done in it, but it is a question of first things first – "

Raina looked at him.

"If you mean what I think you mean," she said, "it is the kindest and nicest thing you could possibly say."

"I am giving away no secrets," the Earl replied, "so you will just have to wait to see what I mean."

She knew, however, that he had been deeply moved by the plight of the people in the village. And he had promised that 'something would be done' and she knew he would keep his word.

The Comtesse was determined not to be left out and she put her hand on the Earl's arm.

"I always find that you keep your word, however difficult it may be," she cooed at him. "But then, *mon cher*, you are a very unusual and wonderful man."

She said the words with such deep expression in her voice that Raina was not surprised that the Earl looked embarrassed and quickly changed the subject.

"What do you want to drink, General?" the Earl asked, looking at the grog table. "I have a distinct feeling it is champagne or water!"

The General laughed.

"Then I will not say no to a glass of champagne, even though it is against my rules."

"What are your rules, General?" Raina asked.

She felt that she must somehow keep the Comtesse out of the conversation.

"My rules are quite simple," the General replied. "I don't drink when I am working and that has meant, for the last year or so, I have been almost a teetotaller!"

Everyone laughed at his admission.

Then Barker announced that luncheon was served and they went into the dining room.

As soon as they sat down, the Earl started to talk to the General about the war and asked what had happened to many of their friends and compatriots.

Actually Nanny and Raina found the conversation extremely interesting, but the Comtesse fidgeted and tried to make the Earl concentrate on her.

'She is overdoing it,' Raina thought. 'If the Earl is wise, he will realise that she is trying to bind him to her with flattery. Surely he will see that she is not sincere.'

As she was saying this to herself, the Earl asked her a question.

As their eyes met, she had a strange feeling that he was reading her thoughts again.

Just for a moment it was impossible to answer him and, as she had been thinking of him and the Comtesse, she had not really heard what he had just said.

"What are you suggesting?" she asked.

"I was wondering whether you would like to ride again this afternoon. I am anxious to see the farms that I understand are untenanted, but I am told that the roads up to them are blocked, which means we will have to ride."

"But you cannot leave me alone," the Comtesse moaned. "How can you be so unkind, Clive, when I have been looking forward to driving with you in the beautiful country lanes?"

For a moment Raina thought he was going to give in to her, but instead the Earl said,

"You must allow me, although it may seem a bit discourteous, to put my estate first. You must remember I have come back here after being away for six long years, and so I have to learn what has happened in my absence."

"But I want to be with you," the Comtesse fretted.

She put her hand on his arm and looked up at him, fluttering her long mascara-darkened eyelashes.

"I will tell you what we will do," the Earl said and Raina knew that he was thinking quickly. "I will ride with Raina to see the farms and, when I come back, I will take you round the picture gallery and the music room with its fine pieces of French furniture."

"That will be lovely and very thrilling for me," the Comtesse said, "but you promise not to be away for long?"

"We will be as quick as we can and I am sure you will find something interesting in the newspapers which have just arrived."

"If we were in Paris, as we were before, you know that there would be so many exciting stories in them," the Comtesse replied, "but, alas, I find the English newspapers so dull. They are never so intimate or as rude about people in the Social world as we are in France."

"A good thing too," the General said unexpectedly. "I disapprove of gossip whether I hear it or read it. The gossip in French newspapers is, in my opinion, a disgrace to cultured and civilised behaviour!"

"I don't know why you say that," the Comtesse protested angrily.

Then they were fighting each other with words, but Raina thought that the General won quite easily.

However, while the argument raged, she looked at the Earl and realised that there was a twinkle in his eyes.

'He cannot really be in love with her,' she reflected, 'if he is amused when she is losing an argument so easily.'

There was no question about it, as the General was cleverly proving his point by quoting the trouble there had been at some defamatory reports in the French newspapers.

One politician had been obliged to resign because of what had been published about him, which actually, the General said, was untrue.

The meal Mrs. Barker had provided for them was simple but very edible and it ended with some local cheese Barker told them had been delivered at the back door only half-an-hour before.

"It's a present for his Lordship," he said, "from the cheese-makers in the next village. They left it with their compliments, saying they were real pleased his Lordship were back."

"How kind of them," the Earl commented.

"I expects your Lordship'll have a great number of presents afore the day be out," Barker went on. "I were told they be cheering you in the village and be decorating some of the cottages so they don't look so bad when your Lordship next sees them."

It was obvious that the Earl was not only surprised but deeply touched and Raina realised that nothing could be more helpful than that the people should express their gratitude when he least expected it.

She hoped he would thank them and the answer to this question came quicker than she anticipated.

The Earl was saying,

"I hope, Barker, you took their names so that I can write to each of them. I will start with the kind people who have given us this excellent cheese."

"It is really delicious," Nanny said. "You will find that the people of this County are always very generous and want to give as well as receive."

"I certainly did not expect to receive presents," the Earl replied. "It makes me feel just as I did when I was a schoolboy, as if I have really come home."

Raina noticed the frown between the Comtesse's beautiful eyes and she knew that she was wondering how she could disparage such a gesture, but there was really nothing she could say.

Instead she put her hand over the Earl's and cooed,

"I have a present to give you for your kindness in bringing me to England, Clive. I am so glad to be here and not on the other side of the Channel, so many miles away."

"Of course we are delighted to have you," the Earl said lightly.

He then rose from the table.

"Come along, Raina," he proposed. "If we are to visit the farms, the sooner we start the better."

"Yes, of course, my Lord, I will go and change if you will see to the horses."

She reached the door and then looked back,

"Unless you are going to grab Sunrise for yourself, I should like to ride him."

She did not wait for the Earl's reply, but ran from the dining room up the stairs to her bedroom.

She thought with satisfaction that the Earl had paid little attention to the Comtesse at luncheon and she had not succeeded in preventing him from visiting the farms.

'She is a horrible woman and the sooner he realises that the better for all of us,' she mused yet again.

It did not take more than a few minutes to change into her riding habit.

She ran back downstairs, tying her hair back tidily as she did not wear a hat. She never wore one when she rode alone and it seemed ridiculous to dress herself up just for the Earl and the empty farms they would be visiting.

The farmers, who had occupied them, had left when they could no longer find suitable labourers, nor could they afford to restock their farms with lambs or cattle on the slender proceeds of their efforts.

When the last farmer had left, he had said to her father,

"I'll never forget how 'appy I've been here. But one can't fight the war and me pockets be just as empty as the fields be."

"What on earth could I say to him?" the Vicar had asked when he returned home. "I merely blessed him and I will naturally include him in my prayers."

Raina had known that her father had longed to give the men some money so that they could stay on, but he had already cut his household expenses to a minimum and there was nothing he could do.

However, she was wondering that if the Earl too was hard up, as he gave her the impression of being, how would the fields ever be sown or the farms re-stocked.

When she reached the stables, she found that she had not asked in vain.

Sunrise had a side saddle on his back.

"Thank you! Thank you!" she enthused to the Earl.

He smiled as he replied,

"You look more attractive on him than I do. I was thinking that the birds, the rabbits and the flowers should admire us since there is no one else to do so."

"That is true, my Lord. I am hoping the day will come when we will put on our best 'bib and tucker' to impress those we are visiting."

The Earl did not answer and she wondered if her saying something so provocative had made him think that the sooner he went away the better.

'I must be careful, very careful not to upset him,' she determined.

She wondered desperately how she could persuade him that nothing could be more marvellous than to see the estate restored to the bountiful prosperity it had enjoyed before the war.

They rode through the garden into the paddock and, when they were in an open field, they let the horses gallop.

Raina knew the Earl wanted to first visit the largest and most productive farm on the estate.

The farmer and his wife had six children and they had been very successful in breeding pedigree cows as well as a new breed of sheep that had caused quite a sensation in the neighbourhood.

One by one their men had left them and, although he worked almost twenty-four hours a day, the farmer had not been able to keep up what in the past had been the finest farm in the whole of the County. He had been admired and praised, but now he could not bear any longer the realisation that his position had changed.

He was no longer respected as he had been before and he had told the Vicar that he was going North.

"Things be much cheaper up there," he said, "and if I gets a small farm I could manage it meself. They won't know me there and they won't expect so much. Me wife's family'll be there as well to 'elp us."

"We will miss you very much," the Vicar said, "and I am sure when the Earl returns he will say the same."

Now when Raina could see the empty farmyard, she found it very difficult to know how to make the Earl understand how productive this farm had once been.

The farm buildings were not quite as dilapidated as some of the others. However, windows had been smashed either by small boys throwing stones or by the elements.

The roofs of some barns had fallen in and the yard was in a bad state with dirt and broken stones.

"I remember coming here when I was a boy," the Earl sighed after he had looked round. "The farmer's wife used to give us gingerbread, which she had made for her own children."

"I enjoyed gingerbread too," Raina said. "Perhaps one day we will come back to find it being made in that nice big kitchen that was always spotlessly clean."

She wondered if the Earl would say he would not be coming back. He did not answer, but merely walked to the next room that had been the farmer's sitting room.

Soot had fallen from the chimney into the room and there was a large stain on the ceiling, which Raina knew meant the roof was leaking. She did not say anything, but she had the idea that the Earl had noted it.

He walked out of the farmhouse in silence and then he helped her onto Sunrise and mounted his own horse.

"Where to next?" he asked.

"The next farm is about a mile away," she replied. "But I warn you the field is very rough and we must not go too fast."

"How often do you ride round here?" he enquired.

"I have been fortunate enough to ride your horses two or three times a week," Raina answered. "Your Head Groom, who as you know is getting old and decrepit, was very grateful to me for giving them the exercise he had difficulty in doing himself. It is only in the last month he has had two boys to help him, but they are not particularly good with animals."

"Surely it was possible to do better than that in the village," the Earl asked almost sharply.

Raina shook her head.

"What wages they were offered were very small, therefore it did not tempt the older men. The boys were pleased to have anything, however little, to spend on food."

There was no answer to this. Mr. Munn could not give them what he did not have.

They went on to the next farm, then to a third and at neither of them did the Earl ask any questions.

He merely looked round, seeing, as Raina had seen so often, that everything that could be broken was broken.

It would be an almost Herculean task to repair all of them and Raina was longing to ask how he thought without doing so he would be able to help the village.

It flashed through her mind once again that the only answer was somehow to sell something in the house.

She had thought a thousand times during the war, and so had her father, that it was cruel to let people almost starve to death when there were thousands of pounds worth of valuables lying idle in The Hall.

War or no war, there were collectors who would be only too pleased to be given a chance to buy one or more of the pictures, but she knew that her father would never cheat or do anything underhand.

She kept wondering now what the Earl would do.

She could, however, definitely not ask him point-blank, because she was sure that he had not yet made up his mind.

They rode home in silence and then Raina said,

"I hope you have not been too unkind to poor Mr. Munn, who did his best, but as he often told Papa, he could not spend what he did not have."

"All I can say in my defence," the Earl replied, "is that I had no idea that matters were as bad as they are."

"I don't think anyone is blaming you personally, my Lord, but now you are back, they believe that you will lead them to a new victory."

She saw the Earl purse his lips and thought perhaps she had said too much.

So she quickly pointed out what a magnificent view of The Hall there was from where they were riding.

The Earl seemed to be thinking very deeply and she was sensitive enough to realise that he had no wish to talk and so they rode on in silence.

She took him to the other side of the estate where there was not a farm, but yet another small village and the cottages looked very much the same as those they had seen in the morning.

At first no one paid any attention as they rode down the main street and then they heard a woman cry,

"It's the lady from the Vicarage and I guess with 'er be 'is Lordship!"

As her strong voice rang out, it seemed to Raina as if people appeared by magic. The doors of the cottages opened and children ran onto the road.

Almost before the Earl and Raina were aware of it, there was a crowd round them.

The women were telling the Earl how much they had suffered and how glad they were that he was back.

"Now you've come 'ome, it'll be different," one of them called out.

Others asked him to look at their houses to see how damp they became when it rained, and several said all that their husbands wanted was to be back on the land working as they had before the war started.

A great number wanted to shake the Earl's hand.

He bent down from his horse and one woman held his hand in both of hers and cried,

"You'll save us, you'll save us now you be 'ome. Please, my Lord, I wants to live a little longer and see me children 'appy."

She was so pathetic in the way she spoke that Raina felt the tears come into her eyes and she was sure that the Earl was moved by all he was hearing.

Then, when they rode off, the villagers cheered him and some of the young women ran beside him shouting,

"Don't forget us, please don't forget us."

As they turned into the field, the Earl asked,

"Are there any more villages? Because I have had as much as I can take for one day."

"Of course you have, my Lord, but I did not expect that anyone would notice us in that little village. In fact I seldom go there unless they send for me, because it is the furthest from home."

"Do they send for you often?"

"Papa always visited anyone who was ill, dying or had a baby. When he was no longer with us, I tried to do the same."

She paused before she added sadly,

"I am afraid I was not as much help as he had been, but at least they knew that someone cared."

"Is that what you are saying to me now, that I have to show I care, Raina."

"I think you do care," Raina answered him in a low voice. "No one could have had the reception you had this morning, and just now, and not care."

"I promise you I do," the Earl murmured.

She knew it was almost a vow and she was sure that he would not go back on his word.

"If you really mean it," she said, "it's the most wonderful thing you could tell me."

"Why do you say that?" he asked.

"Because ever since you have been back you have been talking about leaving, but now, perhaps involuntarily, I think you have committed yourself."

The Earl smiled,

"Which, of course, was very careless of me!"

The horses were now walking as the ground was so heavy and after what seemed a long silence the Earl said,

"Most women would think that all this was none of their business."

"I can hardly think that, when I live amongst them and they love me, just as they want to love you."

"Do you think their love is important, Raina?"

"Of course it is. They are like children. They trust those they consider their betters and believe, just as a child does, that they will not be thrown away or left to starve."

The words seemed to come to Raina without her thinking about them and she could see the Earl draw in his breath and then he stared ahead as if he was looking into the future.

There was silence until they had almost reached the end of the field and then the Earl announced,

"I will think all this over very carefully and decide by the end of the week just exactly what I will do. Will that satisfy you?"

"Only," Raina said after a little pause, "if you give me the answer I am longing and praying for."

"Then you will have to wait," the Earl said almost sharply. "I have to think and I have to plan. There is much more to this than appears on the surface."

Raina looked at him in surprise.

"I don't know what you mean, my Lord."

"Forget it, Raina. I don't want to make you curious. I just want you to wait and give me a chance to think out what for me is a very heavy problem."

"Please can I help you, just as I managed to help you with the first problem you had to face?"

The Earl smiled.

"You certainly did so very successfully and I don't think anyone who dined with us last night had the slightest suspicion that Lady Evelyn was not who she appeared to be."

"And why should they have suspected her of being anyone else?" Raina asked. "You must admit that Nanny looked and played the part beautifully."

"I thought she looked extremely attractive and was perfectly at home with Lord Lewis and the General."

"I like the General," Raina said, "and he said very kind things about Papa."

"I have yet to hear anyone say anything else," the Earl remarked. "If when I die, I have half the appreciation your father has had, I would be a very proud man."

"I only wish he was here now. I know he would help you to solve your problems without much difficulty."

"I think perhaps you will do that for me, Raina, but I don't want to talk about it at the moment."

He moved his horse forward as he spoke and then, without saying anything, they were racing each other over the flat field in front of them.

Only when they reached the end did Raina exclaim triumphantly,

"Sunrise won by a head. You must have seen it."

"Yes, I did see it," the Earl replied. "Only it is not Sunrise who should take the credit, but you. I have never seen a woman who rides better."

"That I won the race is a good omen that I will solve your problems and show you the way to happiness in the future."

"Is that what you really want for me?" he enquired.

"Of course it is, my Lord. I want you to live here, to be happy and to let your people love you and be grateful as I know they will be. I could not ask for anything that would make me happier."

She spoke with a thrill of joy in her voice that just seemed to fly out from her into the sunshine.

She also looked so lovely with her eyes alight and her head thrown back with the excitement of everything that she was saying.

Then, as her voice died away, there was a silence until the Earl said,

"We must go back to The Hall. I promised to take the Comtesse round the picture gallery and I must keep my word."

It seemed for a moment as if the sunshine had gone in and then Raina responded in a matter of fact voice,

"Yes, of course. She will be waiting for you."

They rode into the stables and the Earl dismounted and so did Raina. She patted Sunrise's neck and told him how good he had been and how much she had enjoyed riding him.

She had talked to horses all her life and her father always told her that, if a horse was difficult, the rider must talk to him and make him familiar with his or her voice before they mounted.

She finished telling Sunrise how good he was and then she was aware that the Earl had handed his horse over to the groom and was walking back to the house.

'He is eager to be with the Comtesse,' she thought and her spirits dropped.

Despite what he had said about his people, he was still attracted by that tiresome unpleasant woman who had trumpeted that he was going to marry her.

As Raina left the stables a few minutes later, she was praying that the Earl would see sense and would send the Comtesse back to France.

'She is wicked, selfish and wrong for him,' Raina thought. 'Please God let him realise it before it is too late.'

She knew without anyone telling her that it would be too late if he married the Frenchwoman, too late, despite all he had said, for the house, too late for the estate and too late the people who depended on him.

As Raina walked towards The Hall, she felt as if her footsteps were repeating over and over again,

"*Too late*! Too late! Too late!"

CHAPTER SIX

When the Earl and Raina had ridden away, Nanny turned to the General,

"Now what do you want to do?"

"I want to be with you," he replied.

She smiled.

"I really ought to explore more of the house so that I can tell the Earl what urgently needs to be repaired."

"Are you certain he will do it?" the General asked.

"How can he possibly refuse? All the people are depending on him and for them it is really a case of life or death."

"I only hope he will not disappoint you."

"Raina has been wonderful," Nanny said almost as if she was speaking to herself. "She has tried to take her father's place, which of course was impossible. If it was not for her, it would be far worse than it is."

"You seem to know a good deal about it all, Lady Evelyn. I thought you had only just come down from the North."

Nanny realised that she had made a mistake and so she said quickly,

"Don't let's talk about it now, General. It's all so depressing. Would you like to walk in the garden or visit the picture gallery?"

"I would like to go into the garden and have some fresh air. I am trying to decide whether I will be in London for a year – as I think I told you, they have offered me a major post in the War Office – or whether I will go back to my house in the country and make certain it does not fall into the same deplorable condition as The Hall."

"Come and look at the gardens, General, and then I will pick your brains as to what can be done about them."

They went into the rose garden and, as the sunshine was quite strong, they walked past all the beds overgrown with weeds and sat down under some trees.

"It would be really lovely here," Nanny sighed, "if there were sufficient gardeners to tend these flower beds and the lawns and to rebuild the greenhouses."

"You look like a flower yourself," the General said. "For the moment neither The Hall nor its garden could ask for more."

Nanny laughed.

"I am not at all used to compliments, General, but I assure you that I appreciate them when they come along."

"I have so much more to say than just compliments, Lady Evelyn. Tell me about yourself."

"That is certainly something I have no wish to do," Nanny replied. "I would much rather hear about your life and how you managed to survive the war."

"I can answer that quite easily. I was very lucky. Although there were moments when I thought that I should never see the sunshine again, I survived."

"It must have been very satisfying for your family."

"Unfortunately I don't have one. Being a soldier is a full-time job, so I have never married. And, of course, a great number of my contemporaries are either dead or have disappeared so that I am no longer in touch with them."

"That sounds a sad story, General. I cannot believe that now the war has ended that you will not find life very enjoyable."

"Alone?" the General questioned pointedly.

"You must have friends even if you have forgotten them and I am quite certain that if you are in London for long, you will soon find yourself being invited to dinner parties and balls every night."

Nanny gave a little laugh before she added,

"Every hostess wants a single man, especially one who is so distinguished."

"Now you are thinking of the Earl rather than me! At the balls given in London for all the young *debutantes*, they will look on me as a grandfather."

"I feel sure that you are wrong, General."

There was a long pause and then he said,

"What I really want is someone to share my life with me, especially if I accept the post at the War Office."

Nanny could not reply and the General went on,

"As I have never before asked anyone to marry me, I know I am not doing it very well. But I think you must know what I am trying to say to you, Evelyn."

Nanny looked at him in astonishment.

"I don't understand," she murmured.

"I think you do," the General replied. "I am asking you, although not in flowery language, if you will do me the great honour of becoming my wife."

Nanny gave a gasp.

This was the last turn of events she had expected and she could only stare at the General, finding it hard to believe that he was serious.

"I fell in love with you the moment I saw you and I thought you were indeed the most beautiful woman I have ever seen. But you have so much more than beauty. You have what every man needs – warmth and understanding."

Nanny still did not speak and the General added,

"I will do everything I can to make you happy. I think we will find we have a great number of interests in common, and more than anything else, I have lost my heart utterly and can only lay it at your feet, dearest Evelyn."

"I had no idea you felt – like this," Nanny said in a low hesitating voice.

"I am perhaps jumping my fences too quickly, but I am frightened you will go away back to where you have come from and I will not be able to find you. Perhaps I should have held back, but now I have said what is in my heart and I am waiting for you to tell me if I have a chance of loving you as I wish to do."

"You – really – want me?" Nanny stammered.

"More than I can say in words. I never was cut out to express myself. I only want to say I love you, as I said to myself over and over again last night when I had to leave you."

"You really love me?"

He picked up her hand and put his lips against it.

"I have told you I am not very good with words. I can only say that I did not know that love could be so powerful or happen so quickly."

He kissed her hand very gently, then held it in both of his as he continued,

"I knew as soon as I met you that you are different from any woman I have ever met. And something strange seemed to happen inside me. I wanted you. I wanted you desperately. It was with difficulty I did not tell you so the very moment I first set my eyes on you."

"How could that – possibly happen?"

"I have asked myself the very same question and the answer is, it *has* happened. Nothing anyone can say could make it anything but the truth."

113

Nanny looked away from him.

He felt that her profile by the trees was exquisite.

"I thought when I first saw you," Nanny said, "that you are very good-looking and you look too young to be a General."

"I was, when the war ended, one of the youngest Generals in the Army. And I will be forty-nine next year and I realise that I am missing the most wonderful asset any man could have. That is a wife to love who loves me."

His voice was very deep and then he felt Nanny's fingers quiver in his.

"I know you have never been married," he said. "I will therefore, if you will allow me, teach you about love, which will be the most marvellous thing I have ever done."

There was silence and then Nanny breathed,

"I cannot believe – you are saying all this to me."

"But I am saying it and I am waiting for you to give me an answer."

Again there was silence and then Nanny gave out a little cry,

"I cannot marry you! I have only – just realised it! It is quite impossible!"

The General turned towards her.

"Why impossible?" he asked. "You are not already married?"

"No, it's nothing like that, but I have to say 'no'."

"But why? You have to give me an explanation," the General persisted.

Because she was agitated, Nanny would have taken her hand from him, but he was holding it with both of his and she could not move away.

The air seemed to vibrate between them and after what seemed an incredibly long time, Nanny said,

"I am not – who you think I am."

"That does not surprise me," the General replied, "because I am absolutely certain there is no reason for you to wear a wig."

Nanny turned to look at him wide-eyed.

"You know it's a wig?" she asked.

"It's a very clever disguise," the General answered, "and, of course, it makes you look very much older than I am sure you are."

"So you – realised that," Nanny replied, stumbling over the words.

"I thought, although I could have been mistaken, that you are playing the part of a much older woman to impress the Lord Lieutenant and that tiresome gossip Lady Trowbridge."

For a brief moment Nanny could only stare at him and then she enquired,

"How – could you have guessed it?"

The General's eyes twinkled.

"I trained myself in the Army to be very perceptive and not to accept anything at face value. It was an exercise that has served me in good stead. So I knew, my precious, that you are not entirely who you pretend to be."

"You are clever – far too clever," Nanny sighed, "and you are quite right. What you have said is true."

"I thought that it was," he said with satisfaction. "Clive was correct. Lady Trowbridge is a chatterbox and would undoubtedly have told the whole Social world if she had found Clive alone here with that Frenchwoman."

"That is what he was afraid of."

"How old are you really?" the General asked. "I will guess if you want me to and I don't think that I will be very far from the mark."

"I will be thirty-nine next birthday."

"And I will be just ten years older. So I think we will be a perfectly matched and happy couple!"

Nanny gave a little cry.

"No, no you are going too fast! Please listen to me, General, please try to understand."

"Of course I will listen, but I do understand already why you are wearing that wig and pretending to be Lady Evelyn Locke."

Nanny looked at him with startled eyes.

"Did you guess it," she asked, "or did the Earl tell you?"

"I am using my brain and I thought occasionally when he had to use your name, he stumbled over it and so did Raina. Now suppose, darling, you tell me the truth and promise me that you will never lie to me in the future."

"I am frightened because you are so clever," Nanny said. "But when you know the truth – you will no longer want me."

The General smiled very tenderly.

"Whatever you tell me, you will not frighten me away, if that is what you are thinking."

Nanny unexpectedly took her hand from his and turned away from him.

"If I tell you the truth," she said, "you may think, and you would be quite right, that I am not good enough for you. So please don't say anymore in case you feel it commits you to do something you will not wish to do."

The General smiled.

"Whatever you might say will not alter my feelings towards you. It is you I love and I know whatever you may say we are made for each other. I have found you after I thought for many years that I would never find the right woman to belong to me and me only."

He spoke very simply and very quietly.

It made Nanny feel that she wanted to turn round and throw herself into his arms and she would beg him, whatever he felt when he learnt the truth, not to leave her.

"Tell me," the General said gently. "I promise you I will not run away."

"But you may have to. After all you are a General and a brilliant man and I suspect from something you said last night that if you take the position they want you to take at the War Office, you will end up in the House of Lords."

"Now you are using your imagination or perhaps your perception. But that will not affect us. I love you because you are you and where you come from or what your family name is does not really concern me. All I want is that you should take mine."

Nanny turned round to look at him.

"How can you say that when you are so clever? You know as well as I do that because you are important you should marry someone important too."

"That is exactly what I want to do," the General replied. "I want to marry someone who is more important to me than anyone I have met in my whole life. I have been looking for you and praying that perhaps one day I would find you. When I saw you in the candlelight, I knew I had won another victory."

"How can you say such wonderful things to me?" Nanny asked. "I am so very afraid that when you know the truth, you will wish you had not said them."

The General smiled.

"If you think I am going to lose you after looking for you all these years, you are very much mistaken."

He paused for a moment before he added,

"Come along, my darling one, tell me the truth and then we can talk more comfortably about our future."

'Perhaps,' Nanny thought to herself, 'there will be no future.'

Looking across the garden with unseeing eyes she said in a voice that did not sound like her own,

"I am Nanny to Raina – and have looked after her since she was born. My father was a vet and, although my mother was the daughter of a country Squire, he was not of any particular consequence except that he had served in the Grenadier Guards and had been educated at Eton."

"Where I was," the General cried. "So we have yet another thing in common."

"Now you know the truth of who I am, General, and I will fully understand if you want to take back all that you have said."

The General laughed.

"My darling, do you really think it would matter to me if you were the daughter of a crossing-sweeper or your father was locked up in prison? I love you because you are you, because you are everything I have always wanted and longed for and now I would sooner surrender to an enemy force than lose you – "

He spoke with such sincerity, which made Nanny turn towards him with a radiance that transformed her and it made her even lovelier than she had ever looked before.

"Do you really mean that?" she murmured.

The General put his arms round her and pulled her close to him.

Then, as he kissed her, she knew that there was no need to go on arguing.

He loved her as she loved him.

As he said so eloquently, they had found each other after so many years of waiting.

*

When the Earl had left Raina to take the Comtesse round the picture gallery, as he had promised, she went to the library.

But somehow the books did not attract her as they had done before and, instead of taking volumes from the shelves, she went to the window to gaze out at the garden.

She was still worried in case after all she had said to the Earl and all he had seen today, he would still insist on going away to some foreign country.

Then she would never see him again.

'How can he go? How can I let him go?' she now asked herself.

Then, almost like a dark cloud coming down from the sky, she thought that perhaps the Comtesse had told the truth – they were going to be married and then she would go with him.

It was then that she finally admitted to herself what she had actually known for quite some time – that she was in love.

She loved the Earl.

Of course she loved him.

She loved the way he rode, the way he looked and most of all perhaps because he appealed to her for help.

'I have to help him, I have to,' she told herself.

But she did not know how.

When everyone came in for a late tea, she thought there was a smile of satisfaction on the Comtesse's lips.

Raina felt as if a thousand knives were piercing her heart.

'I love him, I love him,' she told herself as the Earl walked across the room to straighten one of the pictures.

"I tell you what we must do first, Raina," he said unexpectedly. "We must go round the rooms and decide which pictures are to be restored right away. There is one by Rubens that I have just noticed in the picture gallery. It will be past repair if it is not attended to rapidly."

"I know the one you mean, my Lord, and it does need attention, but so do a great number of other objects in the house."

"I know," the Earl replied sharply, "but that picture is one of my favourites and I cannot bear it being in such a state."

'He is really worrying about the house now,' Raina thought and her spirits rose.

It was then that she noticed, which she had not done before, that the General was gazing at Nanny in a strange way and, as he did so, Nanny looked up to him with an expression in her eyes that Raina had never seen before.

'They are in love,' she mused and was excited at the idea, but she was too tactful to say anything.

The Comtesse was now speaking in her affected seductive tone to the Earl and Raina was suddenly aware that she herself was the odd one out.

'No one wants me,' she told herself sadly.

It was sheer agony watching the Comtesse touching the Earl with her long elegant fingers.

Raina suddenly felt she could not stay in the same room with them any longer.

"If you will forgive me," she said, "I have matters to attend to."

No one answered her and, as she reached the door, she thought that neither the Earl nor the General was in the least interested in what she did.

She went out of the house and walked across the Park to her home.

She was thinking about the Earl all the time.

Yet she had a longing to be in her own home rather than his and to see Dickie.

He must have sensed that she was coming to him, as, by the time she had found the key and opened the front door, he was jumping and barking loudly with excitement.

She knelt down to hug him and put her arms round him and then she felt the tears running down her face.

"No one loves me but you," she sighed in a broken little voice.

As if Dickie understood, he licked her face to show that he loved her.

Emily came from the kitchen.

"I wondered what 'e be a-barkin' for," she said. "I might have guessed it'd be you, Miss Raina. It's nice to 'ave you back."

"I am only paying a short visit, Emily. I felt lonely and thought that perhaps Dickie wanted me."

"Dickie's been up to your room every night, miss, to see if you was there. Although 'e's been sleepin' with me, 'e's not thought it right and who's to blame 'im!"

Raina laughed.

"I feel sure you have looked after him beautifully, Emily, and I will be home very soon."

"And Nanny'll be with you, I suppose. Her slipped out without tellin' me she were goin' which I thinks were a bit strange."

"It all happened in a big hurry. The Earl arrived and asked me to show him the house and there was so much to tell him about what had happened while he was away."

"I understand alright that you be enjoyin' yourself up at The Hall, but I can tell you, if it 'adn't been for Dickie, I'd 'ave felt real lonely. It were so quiet with no one to talk to, it didn't seem like it should be."

"No, of course, it did not," Raina agreed. "I can assure you we will be back very soon."

Emily was still grumbling as she went back to the kitchen and Raina walked slowly to her father's study.

She felt as if she could almost see him there sitting at his desk, writing his sermon for next Sunday, but instead there was only the quietness of the empty room.

She sat down in one of the armchairs, taking Dickie in her arms. He was trembling with excitement because she was there and nuzzled his nose against her.

"I love you, Dickie" she sighed. "Perhaps you will be the only one I have to love in the future."

She had a feeling that Nanny and the General had something very much in common and it suddenly occurred to her that if Nanny did marry, she would be completely alone and what was more she would have nowhere to go.

The Earl had said that she could stay at The Hall, but, of course, he had not been serious.

If he married the Comtesse, as she had said he was going to do, they would doubtless close up The Hall and they would either live in France or she would go exploring with him in other parts of the world.

The agony made her almost cry out and then she asked herself,

'How could I be such a fool as to fall in love with the Earl? He is just making use of me for the moment and will never think about me again.'

She felt the tears in her eyes again and then she told herself that she must go back, although she wanted to steal away and hide, she knew that it would upset his plans.

Most of all he would dislike an emotional woman who was asking more of him than he wanted to give her.

'He will surely marry the Comtesse, because she is determined he will do so,' Raina told herself. 'I am a fool to think that I could attract him in the same way.'

She hugged and kissed Dickie and told him that she would be back with him soon and anyway, she would come and see him tomorrow. He seemed to understand her and wagged his tail.

But when she had shut the front door and locked it again, she could hear him whining as she walked across the lawn towards the Park.

'At least someone loves me,' she thought defiantly.

But she knew that it was not enough.

She wanted so much more and it was foolish of her, as foolish as asking for the sun, the moon and the stars, which could never be hers.

*

When Raina reached The Hall, she was about to go upstairs, as it would soon be time to change for dinner.

Then she thought that she would look into the study first to see if the newspapers were there. If they were, she was certain that the General or the Earl would be reading them and they would be able to tell her where Nanny was.

She suspected that the Comtesse would be resting before dinner as she had done the previous evening.

She opened the study door and then she stood still transfixed in complete astonishment.

There were only the General and Nanny there and they were standing by the window.

The General's arms were round Nanny and he was kissing her passionately.

123

For a moment Raina just stared at them.

Then, realising they were unaware of her presence, she quietly closed the door and moved away.

She went up to her room.

Now she knew that she had been right in thinking that she would lose Nanny.

It was, of course, wonderful for Nanny and Raina liked the General very much.

'They will be very happy,' she thought, 'but I am quite right when I reckon that the only one left for me is Dickie.'

She had not been in her room long when the door opened and Nanny looked in.

"I was wondering where you were," she began.

"I am here," Raina said unnecessarily.

Nanny walked towards her.

"I have something to tell you, dearie."

"I think I can guess what it is, Nanny, but tell me."

As she looked up at Nanny, she realised that her eyes were shining and she looked quite different from the way she usually did.

In fact she was beautiful.

"The General has asked me to marry him," Nanny cried. "Oh, Raina, I am so happy and I cannot believe it's true."

"I like him. I like him very much, Nanny, and I am sure he will take great care of you."

"That is what he wants to do and it is all like a dream and I am afraid I will wake up and it's not true."

"But it is and, darling Nanny, I want you to be very happy."

"That is what I want for you too, dearie."

Because she felt that she might ask her questions, Raina remarked quickly,

"One at a time! I hope I can be a bridesmaid at your wedding."

"I certainly would not be married without you and we are to be married very quietly in the Church where the General was baptised and where his house is."

Raina wanted to cry out,

'Please don't leave me so soon!'

But she knew it would be selfish.

Nanny was looking so radiant and so happy that it would be wrong.

"Of course," Nanny was now saying, "Charles and I would have no intention of abandoning you. If you have nowhere else to go, then, of course, you must live with us."

"I am sure that is something you would not want immediately. I will stay at the Vicarage. At any rate until the Earl appoints a new Vicar."

"You must talk about it with Charles," Nanny said. "He understands that you are trying very hard to persuade the Earl to stay here and restore the house and the estate."

"I am doing my best," Raina sighed.

It then flashed through her mind that she might tell Nanny what the Comtesse had said, but she thought, at this moment, it would be a mistake.

Nanny was obviously concentrating on the General because she loved him and he loved her.

'They don't want to know about the troubles that will arise if the Earl does go away,' Raina said to herself. 'Which is what I am sure he will do, if he marries that horrible woman.'

But aloud she said,

"I am very happy you have found someone to love and who loves you, Nanny dearest. And just as you have always looked after me and been so wonderful, you will now look after the General."

"I think actually," Nanny added a little shyly, "he reckons he will be looking after me."

"Then you must tell him how clever you are, how efficient and how you have always been marvellous to me ever since I was born."

"I intend," Nanny asserted, "to be looking after you until you marry. As I have already said, Charles is only too willing to have you in his house in Dorset and I know we will be very very happy all together."

Raina did not argue, but she was sensible enough to realise that two people who were very much in love did not want a third person on top of them all the time.

'If I was being married,' she told herself, 'I would want to be alone with the man I loved to talk only to him.'

Then once again there was that pain within her as she thought of the Earl married to the Contesse.

'I hate her! I hate her!' she told herself violently and once again endless daggers were piercing her heart.

Dinner was a rather gloomy meal, as the Comtesse insisted on monopolising the Earl and she made it almost impossible for him to speak to anyone else.

The General and Nanny seemed to be happy talking to each other either with or without words.

Raina again felt very much the one left out.

As soon as the dinner was finished and they moved into the drawing room, she said that she had a headache and went upstairs to her bedroom.

It was with difficulty she prevented herself from crying into the pillow.

She felt totally alone and thought it was something she would be for the rest of her life.

Even if the Earl stayed at The Hall instead of going abroad after marrying the Comtesse, she would make very sure that they entertained only those she approved of.

And she would make absolutely certain that Raina was not invited to The Hall under any pretext.

Raina told herself she might still be able to see him if he allowed her to ride his horses as she had always done, but then the Comtesse would try to stop that too.

Because, like all men, he would prefer a quiet and peaceful life, he would submit to his wife, rather than feel bound in any way to anyone else.

"I love him, I adore him," Raina shouted out in the darkness.

But it was unlikely there would be any response from the stars or from the moon creeping up the sky.

She then tried to go to sleep, but she found herself listening for the others to come upstairs.

Nanny was the first and Raina heard her talking in a low voice to the General before she went into her room and next she could hear the General going into his on the other side of the corridor.

Then Raina heard the Comtesse's voice talking to the Earl as they came up the stairs and they appeared to be arguing.

At first the Comtesse's tone was rather sharp, as if she was disagreeing with something he had said to her and then it changed back to soft and seductive.

Although Raina could not hear just what she was saying, she knew that she was trying to persuade the Earl into doing something she wanted and which he did not.

The voices faded a little, but they were still talking outside the Comtesse's bedroom.

Then Raina heard two doors closing one after the other and they had obviously both retired to bed.

'Now I must go to sleep,' she told herself firmly.

But sleep would not come.

Instead she went to the window to gaze out at the garden below and the stars overhead.

Then she began to pray, almost as if her father was listening, that the Earl would not marry the Comtesse and would by some miracle get rid of her.

"I love him. I adore him," she told the stars. "I love him and I want him to love me. Please, Papa, help me as you have helped other people and make him want me."

Then it seemed to her that her father was very close to her and was hearing her prayer.

She thought that he was telling her, as he had often done in the past, that she must pray to God for help and should do so in Church.

She had been quite small when once she had been very naughty and he had sent her to the Church to pray for forgiveness.

After that she had gone there automatically with all her troubles. She had knelt in front of the altar and asked God to help and guide her.

As the Church was now opened only occasionally for a Service on a Sunday, she had not gone there so often since her father's death and she told herself that her father was rebuking her for not doing so.

It was then she remembered the Chapel downstairs. It might now be in bad repair, but it had been sanctified.

A great number of the Earl's ancestors had been Christened and married there, and she had also learnt from one of the books she had read that the previous Earls had lain in State in the Chapel for two days before they were buried in the family vault in the village Church.

'I will go down to the Chapel now,' Raina decided.

She was walking to the door when she remembered that she had locked the Chapel and taken away the key.

She had meant to hand it over to Mr. Munn, but had forgotten. Instead she had put it in one of the drawers of her dressing table.

She found it and then quietly opened the door of her room.

There was a little light coming from the hall, yet it was easy for her to reach the end of the corridor.

There was a narrow staircase leading down to the floor below and the Chapel and, when she reached the Chapel door, there was a faint light from the glass window above it and it enabled her to put the key in the lock and to open the door.

In the Chapel itself she could see quite clearly.

The moonlight was streaming through the window in which the glass had fallen out and she walked the short way up the narrow aisle.

For a moment it did not matter that the gold cross was almost black and the candles were unlit.

The moonlight was soft and silvery and it gave the whole Chapel a look of mystery.

Raina knelt in front of the altar and the sanctity of the Chapel made it seem very different from every other room in the house.

It was then she felt that, if she prayed, her prayers would be heard and perhaps God would bless her as He had blessed her in the past.

'Help me, God, help me,' she prayed, 'to make the Earl stay and look after the people who believe in him and who need him and make him see the truth and know those who are his true friends and those who are not.'

The prayer seemed to come into her mind almost as if it was being dictated to her.

Then she was suddenly aware of footsteps outside the door. There was no carpet in the passage, only the bare boards and the footsteps, although faint, were clear.

She stopped praying and wondered who it could be.

Then she heard the door that opened into the garden being unlocked and it flashed through her mind that maybe the Earl had come down and was going out for a walk.

Next, although she could hardly believe she was not dreaming, she heard a voice speaking in French.

In fact there were two voices, one a man's voice and the other a woman's.

She was almost sure, although the voice was very low, that the woman's was the Comtesse.

Then she heard footsteps again coming towards the Chapel door.

She had left it ajar and knew that she must hide.

Swiftly she moved forward and then crept under the altar behind the stained and wet cloth that covered it.

Once she was completely hidden, she was aware that the Chapel door was being pushed open.

She heard the Comtesse saying in French,

"Come in here. No one will overhear us and I am delighted to see you – "

CHAPTER SEVEN

Raina held her breath as the Comtesse came into the Chapel.

Then she heard heavier footsteps behind her.

There was a piece of the altar cloth that had worn very thin when the rain had dripped onto it and now, when she knelt up a little straighter, she could see through it in the moonlight the Comtesse standing just inside the door.

There were three men with her.

It was difficult to see them, as they were wearing dark clothes and one of them kept his hat on.

But they looked too short and slim to be English and when they started to speak, Raina realised that they too were French.

"No one saw you come in here?" the Comtesse now asked with an anxious note in her voice.

"*Non, non, madame,*" one of the men replied, "and your maid was very good in telling us all we needed to know."

"She told you about the lake," the Comtesse asked.

"*Oui*, and we have already been there."

The Comtesse gave what Raina thought was a sigh of relief and then she said,

"First things first, tell me when you arrived."

"Very early this morning," one answered. "And we have anchored near London Bridge."

"Oh, yes, I do know where that is," the Comtesse exclaimed, "now what about the will?"

"We went to the Solicitor where you told us to go."

"Monsieur Loyer," she replied. "I am sure he was very helpful."

"He is going to charge you two thousand francs, *madame*," the same man said.

The Comtesse shrugged her shoulders.

"That was inevitable, but he has done it well?"

"Exactly as you told us, *madame*," the man replied. "Monsieur le Comte has left you everything he possesses."

"Including all the money in America?"

"*Oui, oui*," was the reply, "also some money that Monsieur Loyer found in Switzerland. In fact everything Monsieur le Comte owns."

"That is good and the signature was well done?"

"Monsieur Loyer copied it exactly. It is identical to the signature you gave us, *madame*."

The Comtesse, Raina thought, gave a small sigh of satisfaction.

Then she asked,

"And the wedding?"

The diminutive Frenchman, who was doing all the talking, laughed.

"It was perfect, *madame*. Josephina Léon acted as you better than when she was on the stage."

"And the man?" the Comtesse asked.

"We arranged with Felix Marc, who as you know is a success at *Les Folies Bergéres*."

"*Oui, oui*, I remember him. And he looked just like Monsieur le Comte?"

"He wore the uniform Monsieur threw away before he left Paris. No one would have known he was not an Englishman when he took his vows."

"The Priest was not suspicious?"

"*Non, non.* He addressed him most politely as 'my Lord' and when they both signed the Register, they had practised many hours to make sure they did it *exactement.*"

"You have certainly done very well," the Comtesse said, "and I am very grateful to you, Henri."

"You must congratulate both Eduard and André as well," Henri replied. "They have worked very hard too."

"I am grateful to you all," the Comtesse said, "and you will find, once his Lordship is dead, that I will be very generous."

"We have been to the lake," Henri added, "and we have found a place in the wood just before the trees come to an end where his horse will fall."

"You are quite certain of that?" the Comtesse asked almost sharply.

"Quite certain, *madame.* Then we will seize hold of Monsieur and hold him in the lake until he drowns. When he is found, everyone will assume that his horse threw him into the water and he could not escape."

"*Très bon,*" the Countess exclaimed. "As Monsieur always goes to the lake early you must be sure to be there at about six-thirty."

"You can leave it all in our hands, *madame,*" Henri said. "Everything is arranged and, as soon as Monsieur is drowned, a carriage will be there waiting to take us back to London as swiftly as it is possible to travel."

"You are very wise, Henri, as it is always a mistake to hang about once the deed is done."

"I am aware of that and I assure you, *madame*, we never linger because that can be dangerous."

"Well, all I can say once again is that I am very grateful to you all and I will make sure that Monsieur rides to the lake tomorrow morning as he always does."

"And that will be the last time," Henri replied with a sneering laugh.

"I will see you in Paris," the Comtesse added. "I too will leave early tomorrow morning before the tragedy of Monsieur's death is discovered. In fact I will leave on the first ship from London."

"You will come with us, *madame*."

"*Non, non*. From this moment on I don't know you and have nothing to do with you. Officially, of course, that is. When I arrive in Paris and you join me, my gratitude will be waiting for you."

"We are looking forward to that," Henri replied. "And, *madame*, you do understand that there will also be some expenses."

"*Oui, oui*," the Comtesse agreed. "Everything will be paid, but, from this moment until you come to me in Paris, I have no knowledge of you or your whereabouts."

"That is very sensible of you, *madame*."

"Thank you again," she said and held out her hand.

Henri bowed over it.

And then the two other Frenchmen did the same.

"Now be careful that you move back in the shadow of the trees," the Comtesse advised. "No one is likely to be awake at this hour of the night, at the same time it would be a great mistake for anyone to notice you."

"*Oui, oui, madame*, we understand," Henri replied. "*Au revoir* and *merci bien* for all you have promised us."

Again he raised her hand formally to his lips and the other two men bowed and murmured,

"*Bon soir, madame.*"

Then they moved out into the corridor.

Raina heard them open the door that led into the garden and the Comtesse followed them to lock the garden door behind them and bolt it.

Then she passed the Chapel, leaving the door ajar as it had been when she arrived.

For one awful moment Raina had been afraid that she might close it and turn the key in the lock, in which case she would have great difficulty in escaping.

Because she wanted to be certain that the Comtesse was upstairs and back in her bedroom, she did not move for the next five minutes.

Instead she prayed to her father and thanked him for telling her to go into the Chapel.

And then she prayed to God and thanked Him for giving her the chance of saving the Earl's life.

'No wonder I thought the Comtesse was wicked,' she reflected. 'It is no wonder I felt repelled by her the moment I saw her. She is evil and the Earl must learn what she is planning as soon as I can reach him.'

She knew, however, it would be a ghastly mistake if the Comtesse suspected for a single moment that she had been overheard.

Raina knew she must tell the Earl what was planned for tomorrow morning, yet he might think she was merely imagining things. Supposing he would believe nothing she alleged against the Comtesse?

'Nevertheless, I have to warn him,' she determined. 'Then if he takes other men with him, all armed, he will be able to protect himself.'

135

At last, feeling cramped as she had been enclosed in such a small space, she crawled out from under the altar.

Then she knelt and thanked God once again that she could save the Earl.

'How anyone could be so wicked as to murder him for everything he possesses?' she asked herself.

She shuddered at the terrible thought of what might have happened if she had not come down to the Chapel, and she was certain it was a Power greater than herself that had led her there at exactly the right moment.

She said a further prayer of thanks before she rose from her knees and walked towards the door.

She turned the key in the lock, but she did not take it away.

'It would be wrong,' she thought, 'to do so, as, if the door of the Chapel had not been open, the Comtesse might have gone elsewhere to discuss her evil plans and I would not have overheard them.'

She went up the stairs making certain that her feet made no sound.

When she stepped out into the corridor, there was no one to be seen.

By now she was quite certain that everyone would be asleep, including the Earl.

She tiptoed to the door of the Master suite.

Thinking that it would be a mistake to knock, she opened the door quietly.

The curtains were drawn back and the moonlight was pouring in through the bow window at the far end of the room.

In the moonlight she walked to the large canopied four-poster bed.

Then she stopped dead – there was no one in it.

Next she could hear slight sounds coming from the bedroom next door.

It was where the Comtesse was sleeping.

As she turned she could see that the communicating door between the two bedrooms was open.

Now she knew it was impossible for her to speak to the Earl tonight and so she would have to wait until the morning.

Carefully she retraced her steps and slipped out of the door and into the passage shutting it quietly behind her.

As she reached her room and remembered where the Earl was, she shuddered at the mere thought of what was happening.

'How can he be attracted by a woman like that,' she asked herself.

Then because of what she had heard, she climbed into bed and hid her face in the pillow.

She did not expect to sleep, but she did doze for a little while.

*

When the stars began to disappear one by one and the first streak of light came from the East, she got up and dressed.

Raina knew that there was no need to hurry because the Earl never rode before seven o'clock.

She did not want to stand in the stables waiting for him and it was unlikely there would be any sign of a groom until it was time to get the Earl's horse ready for him.

At the same time she knew that she must not make anyone suspicious.

She had actually forgotten that the Comtesse had brought with her, quite naturally, a French lady's maid. It was she who had told the Frenchmen by which door they could enter the house without being seen to enable them to talk to the Comtesse.

It must have been she who had unbolted the garden door and the Comtesse had only to turn the key to open it.

What was more, Henri had said that she had been very useful in telling them where the lake was and how the Earl invariably rode there every morning.

'She must not see me,' Raina decided.

Finally, when it was almost six-thirty, she crept out of her room.

She went down the backstairs, which led to a door that was seldom used.

There appeared to be no one about.

Then she went into the stables and to her surprise she saw a sleepy Ned putting a bridle on Sunrise.

"Good morning, Ned," she said. "Did his Lordship order Sunrise for him to ride this morning?"

"Oh, it be you, Miss Raina," he answered. "No, 'is Lordship's taken Firefly."

"Taken!" Raina exclaimed. "What do you mean?"

"'E tells I to get Sunrise ready for you and 'e goes orf as I tells you on Firefly," Ned replied.

Raina felt as if her heart stood still.

Then she took hold of Sunrise's bridle and led him as quickly as she could out of the stables and into the yard.

"You forgot your saddle, Miss Raina," Ned called after her.

Raina did not answer.

She flung herself onto Sunrise's back pulling up her riding skirt as she sat astride him.

Then she forced him forward and they sped out of the yard and into the paddock, while Ned stared after her in disbelief.

Kicking Sunrise with her heels, Raina rode him far faster than she had ever ridden him before.

She thought, as they rushed over the fields, that her heart had stood still and she could only pray frantically that she would be in time.

She reached the field that led down to the wood.

Then she could see the Earl ahead of her silhouetted against the trees. He was actually trotting fairly slowly as if he was in no hurry, but even so he was still quite some distance from her.

Raina thought that it would be a mistake to shout, as the men in the far side of the wood might hear her.

She merely kicked Sunrise again and told him, in a voice that did not sound like her own,

"Hurry! Hurry!"

There was, she was to think later, such a desperate feeling within her that it made the Earl turn and look back just before he rode into the wood.

As he saw her galloping towards him, he drew in Firefly and they stood waiting for her to reach them.

As Raina then drew Sunrise to a standstill, the Earl stared at her in amazement.

She was riding astride! And without a saddle!

He also saw the expression on her face.

"What's the matter? Why are you up so early?" he demanded.

Finding every word difficult, Raina blurted out,

"Come away – from the wood. I have something – to tell you – something that deeply concerns you."

The words seemed to jerk from between her lips.

Then the Earl asked,

"What has upset you, Raina? What has happened?"

"Come away from here – quickly!"

There was a small copse a little to their left and she led the way until they were among the trees.

Now they could not be heard, she reckoned, by the men waiting for the Earl and it was impossible for them to see them because they were on a lower level.

But Raina was still afraid the Comtesse's lady's maid might have seen her leave The Hall and she might then manage to tell the men that their victim was not alone.

Now, as Raina and the Earl drew up under the trees in the copse, she felt able to speak.

The Earl spoke first,

"What is going on? What is all this about?"

"That is just what I am going to tell you," Raina replied. "Why, oh why, did you leave so early?"

"I find that difficult to answer, as I am waiting to hear what has upset you so."

Slowly she told him what had happened last night.

He listened to her without interrupting until she had finished.

Then he asked,

"Why did you not come and tell me after the men had gone?"

For the first time since she had been speaking Raina looked away from him and he saw the colour come into her cheeks.

"I went to your room, but you were not there."

"The Comtesse called me into hers," the Earl said, "and gave me a cross that she said was blessed and which she

140

asked me to throw into the lake this morning. She was sure that it would bring us both luck if it was in the lake I love."

"That was to make sure that you went there."

"I realise that now, but she was insistent it would bring us both good luck. Although I doubted it, I had no reason to refuse her request."

"No, of course not, but in doing so you would have – *died*."

Raina's voice broke on the last word.

Then the Earl said in a very different tone,

"Now we must act and quickly. I need three strong men. Do you know where I can find them."

Raina knew there was no one particularly strong at The Hall.

For a moment she was silent, then gave a little cry.

"Of course, I know who you want! They live in the village at the carpenter's house and the shed he works in is near my home. He is a big man and has two fit sons and they have just returned, as you have, from the Army of Occupation."

"Show me the way to them – now!"

They galloped across the fields keeping out of sight of the house as much as possible.

As they rode through the Park, Raina could see her own house in the distance.

The Earl saw it too and said,

"I am not having you mixed up in this mess. Show me where these men are, then go home, Raina, and wait for me. I will come and tell you what has happened as soon as it is all over."

"Will you promise you will?" Raina asked. "I will be praying you are safe and they don't hurt you."

"They will not hurt me. I will take great care."

"You promise, you really promise," she begged.

Their eyes met and he added very gently,

"I would never break any promise I make to you."

Then he turned quickly and rode off to the house that Raina had pointed out to him.

She knew the carpenter was a strong man. His sons were all tall and athletic. They had always won any races that were held in the village and, as soon as they came out of the Army, they had repaired their own home and anyone else's who could afford to pay them, which were not many.

She felt certain that under the Earl's direction they would be able to cope with the Frenchmen, who, as far as she could see in the Chapel, had not been any taller than the Comtesse.

She put Sunrise into the Vicarage stable and then went into the house.

Dickie must have sensed she was there and came rushing to welcome her.

She went first up to her bedroom and took off her riding clothes and, because it was so hot, she put on a thin cotton dress.

Then talking to Dickie she went into her father's study.

On one wall was a very beautiful crucifix which he had brought back from Rome when he was a young man and in front of it was a *prie-dieu*, which had been given to him by a grateful parishioner.

Raina knelt down on it and prayed frantically as she had never prayed before that the Earl would be safe.

She knew that he was completely determined to tackle the Frenchmen, but she was afraid they might either shoot or knife him.

'Please God, please keep him safe and don't let him be hurt,' she prayed over and over again.

Yet somehow she was sure he would be the winner.

He was cleverer than they were.

*

It seemed to her as if she had prayed for hours and hours, but it was actually less than an hour later that Dickie growled.

Then she heard footsteps in the hall and knew that the Earl had come in through the front door which she had left open.

Jumping to her feet she ran down the passage and found him.

As she expected, he was standing in the hall as if waiting for her.

"Are you safe? Are you all right? Have they hurt you?" she cried.

The words seemed to fall from her.

As his arms went round her, his lips came down on hers.

For a moment Raina could not believe what was happening.

Then his kisses became more demanding and more passionate and she felt the wonder of it seep through her as if she was touched by the sun itself.

The Earl's arms were very strong and he pulled her closer and closer still to him.

He went on kissing her as she felt her whole body melt into his and that she was a part of him.

Then he raised his head.

"My darling," he breathed, "how were you clever enough to save me."

"What has happened? Tell me what has happened,"

143

she gasped.

The Earl looked round.

"I think that we should talk in a more comfortable place."

Raina realised they were still standing in the hall.

"Come into Papa's study. It is where I was praying for you."

"I thought you would – "

They went into the study and when he shut the door he took her into his arms and kissed her again.

It seemed a long time before they sat down side by side on the big sofa.

"You are safe, you are really safe and that is all that matters," Raina said breathlessly.

"All thanks to you, my darling Raina, but it might have been a very different story."

"Tell me what happened," she pleaded.

"I found the three men you told me about and when I told them what was intended, they were all horrified but only too eager to help me. I thought there was no time to lose even though it was only just after seven o'clock when we started back. I was riding and there were two men on the carpenter's horses and one running."

"I thought you might have to walk and that would have taken longer."

"I was anxious to catch them before they gave up and decided to try again tomorrow."

"And you – did," Raina murmured.

"We did," he replied, "and we gave them a little of their own medicine."

"What did you do?" she asked.

"We took them by surprise, having left our horses

outside the wood. We threw all three of them into the lake as they had intended for me. They very nearly drowned, but were conscious enough to understand when I spoke to them."

"What did you say?"

"I told them that I could have them imprisoned and doubtless transported, but, as we are a merciful nation, and had not completely slaughtered their Army at Waterloo, so I would give them another chance of life."

"You let them go?" Raina gasped.

"I did not want a scandal," the Earl said gently. "Nor, my darling, did I want you to be involved in it."

"So you let them go?" Raina repeated.

"I told them if they were found on English soil or sea by the end of the day, I would send the Police for them. As they were still soaking wet and somewhat bemused, we put them in the carriage that was waiting to take them back to London."

Raina gave a murmur, but the Earl went on,

"We told the driver where to take them. If they gave him any trouble on the way or did not board the ship, he was to notify the Police."

"Do you think they will do that?"

"I think they will be glad to leave England at once and that is the only thing that matters."

"What really matters is that you are alive," Raina sighed. "How could anyone have thought of such a ghastly way for you to die?"

She realised she was speaking of the Comtesse and she looked away from him, the colour rising in her cheeks.

"I know what you are thinking," he said, "and I will tell you one thing. I fell in love with you when you first said you would help me and I knew that everything you were telling me was right."

"You – loved – me?" Raina stammered.

"I knew then that you were everything I had been looking for and longing for, but had never found."

"But the Comtesse?"

"I swear to you on everything I hold sacred," the Earl answered, "that when I fell in love with you, I never touched her again."

He paused for a moment before he added,

"I told her I had strained myself while out riding and it was impossible to make love to her. Although she resented it, there was nothing she could do."

"But she was – planning to murder – you. How – could anyone be so wicked?" Raina whispered.

"She wanted my money. By some accident, which I need not go into, she learnt that my father had made a fortune for me in two other countries."

Raina stared at him.

"A fortune!" she exclaimed.

"Quite a considerable one. He invested it for me when I was eighteen and told me I was to swear to him on the Bible that I would not touch it for ten years."

Raina gave a little sigh, but the Earl went on,

"He was a very astute man. He was sure that in ten years, especially with the war against Napoleon developing as it was at that time, we would need the money. While other countries that were not involved in the war would be very much richer than we would be in England."

"So it was true when the Comtesse spoke about the money you have invested in America and Switzerland?"

"Indeed and as it happens, the ten years will be up next month."

Raina stared at him and from the expression in her eyes he knew what she was asking him.

"It will all be spent," he said, "just as you want it to be spent, on the house, on the estate and, of course, on the people who love you and I hope will eventually love me."

"Oh, Clive, is that – really true?" Raina asked.

Her voice broke.

"My precious, you are not to cry about it," the Earl said. "Everything is all right now. I was a fool, I know, to let that woman come back to England with me. But she amused me when I was in Paris and, when she insisted, I suppose I was too weak to be firm and leave her behind."

"But all the time – she was planning and scheming to steal your money – and murder you," Raina murmured.

"Forget it. It's over and we have won. Our victory, my darling, means that you can put into operation all the things you have told me I must do. But first of all, before you do anything else, you must marry me."

"Oh, Clive, you are – quite certain that I am good enough for you?" Raina cried.

"You are much, much too good for me," he replied, "and I will tell you, when we are married, how lovely you are and how much I love you and how my whole world revolves around you."

He pulled her a little closer to him before he added,

"We have such an enormous amount to do and the sooner we start the better."

"I agree but, darling Clive, are you quite, quite sure that you really want me? I don't think I would ever be as attractive as the Comtesse."

"Forget her! She was just a ship that passed in the night and she never meant what you mean to me."

"I cannot believe I am not dreaming. I will wake up and find that I am alone in the Vicarage and I have not even seen you since you were a boy!"

"I will make certain that I am very real and much more demanding than any boy could be!"

Raina gave a little laugh.

"I love everything you say and I so love being with you. I was afraid, very afraid, that you would marry the Comtesse and I would be all alone."

"I never had the slightest intention of marrying her, even if I had never met you. That was why she had to stoop to such desperate lengths to get her greedy hands on my money."

He pulled Raina closer to him before he breathed,

"Forget her and forget all the ugly and unpleasant events that have happened, just as I want to forget the war. I was foolish to believe that someone like the Comtesse could make me forget the horrors I had seen at Waterloo."

"I know it must have hurt you that so many horses died in the battle."

"It was terrible and I don't want to think about it."

The Earl kissed her before he declared,

"What we have to think about, my precious, is us. Now can you arrange for the Parson of the next Parish to marry us, tomorrow if possible?"

"As quickly as that?" Raina laughed.

"The carpenter and his sons have told me that they will work today and all night and the Chapel will be ready early tomorrow morning."

Raina gave a little gasp.

"We are to be married – there?"

"Of course. Otherwise we would need a Special Licence and I don't intend to wait that long!"

He saw the surprise on her face and he said slowly,

"All we need are the flowers from your garden to make the Chapel look as it should do. A bower of beauty for you, Raina!"

"And we really can be married – tomorrow?"

"Do you suppose I can wait for you, my darling. I suggest instead of going away on our honeymoon, we must start work here immediately?"

There was definitely a question mark in his voice.

Raina was still before she replied,

"I think, darling Clive, that we could go away for a week, perhaps in your father's yacht. I understand it is still in good repair although no one has used it."

"Do you mean it? I really had forgotten it existed."

"Your father took me on his yacht when peace was announced. We sailed up to Northumberland and it was the most exciting trip I have ever been on. Unfortunately, your father was not at all well and spent most of the time in his cabin."

"That definitely is what we will do, Raina. So we will be together and I will tell you how much I love you, and we will compete with Nanny and the General as to who loves whom the most!"

He kissed her and it was impossible to think of anything else.

At last Raina gently pushed him away.

"You do realise that we have not had any breakfast yet? And I don't suppose Emily realises we are here."

"I think we should go back to The Hall," the Earl said. "We have a great deal of planning to do and actually I told the carpenter and his sons to meet me at ten o'clock."

"Are you really expecting them to start work at once?" Raina asked.

"He seems a sensible man and he told me that his brother has a much larger business in the town, which is, as you know, only three miles away."

"That is brilliant of you. You will be employing the people from the villages rather than a smart firm from London."

"I am sure I would hate a smart firm from London," the Earl said. "I want people I can trust and, as you say, my darling, who will restore The Hall with love."

Because she could not think of anything more to say, Raina kissed him.

Immediately his arms were round her and then he was kissing her wildly, passionately as if he was half-afraid he would lose her.

Then when they rode back side by side to The Hall, Barker was waiting on the doorstep for them.

"I wondered where you'd gone, my Lord, as you were so late this morning," he began.

"I was afraid we might have missed our breakfast," the Earl replied. "But please tell Mrs. Barker we are both starving."

"I thinks I should inform your Lordship," Barker said, "that your guest, the Comtesse, has left."

Raina slipped her hand into the Earl's.

"Left?" the Earl asked. "Why did she leave?"

"I'm not sure, my Lord, but her lady's maid, who'd gone for a walk, came back in a hurry and asked if a groom would drive her Mistress to the nearest Posting inn as she had to return to London immediately."

It was obvious that Barker was curious as to why there was so much haste.

It was only when they were alone having breakfast that Raina reminded the Earl that she had overheard the

Comtesse saying in the Chapel that she intended to leave before the tragedy was discovered.

"I remember you telling me," the Earl exclaimed.

"Do you think she will now go back to France on the ship the three men came in?" Raina asked.

"I imagine so, but it does not concern either of us, my darling one. We have won a very difficult and a very peculiar battle."

"That is true, Clive, and love has finally conquered war and may it always be the same for everybody for the rest of our lives," Raina sighed.

"Now, we have to celebrate our victory by putting everything into operation you have told me has to be done and the quicker the better."

Raina laughed.

"I felt certain you would say that, it is so like you. You always want everything in a hurry. But I think this is going to take us a long time."

"A long time of happiness," the Earl said, "and that reminds me I have not kissed you for at least ten minutes."

He bent towards her and kissed her.

Then, because their kisses were so wonderful, they clung to each other.

They made Raina feel so excited that she hid her face against his shoulder.

"As soon as we are married," the Earl was saying, "we will go to London and pick up my father's yacht. By the time we come back, I feel sure Munn and all the others will have put everything into operation for us."

"They will not be able to manage without you."

"They will have to," the Earl replied. "I am going to have a honeymoon whatever else I may give up. That, my darling, is not my so-called freedom, but the journeys I have always wanted to make to distant parts of the world."

"Will you be very miserable – if you cannot travel," Raina asked a little hesitatingly.

"I don't want to go anywhere in the world unless you are with me, but first things first. When you are really content and pleased with The Hall and everything round it, when everyone in all the villages have rosy cheeks and fat tummies, because they are eating so much, then we might go off to some secret exciting places together. I will show you the world that has always attracted me, but not half as much as I am attracted to you!"

Raina gave a little cry and put her arms around his neck.

"I love you, I adore you," she cried. "God Himself has answered all my prayers. I thought you would either desert The Hall and I would never see you again or you would marry the Comtesse – or both!"

"You have indeed saved me from both calamities and one thing you can be quite certain of is that we will always do what *you* want."

He paused for a moment before he added,

"And that is something I will teach our children."

"Oh, darling Clive," Raina cried, "if they are half as wonderful as their father, that is all I ask,"

"And, of course, the girls must be as beautiful as their mother,"

Then the Earl was kissing her again, kissing her until she felt that he was carrying her up into the sky and they were touching the stars.

God had answered her prayers and they were both blessed.

Their love, which came from God, would guide and protect them all their lives until they reached Heaven.